D0711255

Bogota Public Library
375 Larch Avenue
Bogota, NJ 07603

"A stranger walks into town · Lyrical and blindingly clear, Ben Ehrenreich's *Ether* unfolds in dreamy simultaneous timescapes punctuated by flashes of violence. Moving between busses and bars, rail yards and suburbs, Ehrenreich's novel depicts the teeming activity that persists in the world beneath an ether of numbness. Like a David Lynch movie transcribed by Pierre Reverdy, it's a brilliant and unforgettable book, written somewhere between sleeping and waking." — Chris Kraus author of *Torpor* and *Where Art Belongs*

"A book that's both pure as snow and filthy as dirt, with the lovely detachment of ice. Like Beckett, Ehrenreich has the talent of being particular and general at once, and thus steps outside time." — Lydia Millet, Pulitzer Prize finalist for *Love in Infant Monkeys*

"Ben Ehrenreich's *Ether* is anything but. The descriptions pop. The world is rendered without qualification, without fear. The structure is challenging, refreshing, effective. This is an intense, intelligent novel novel that paints a vivid picture of an America that most of us refuse to see, are afraid to see. This is real art." — Percival Everett, author of *I Am Not Sidney Poitier*

"*Ether* is a dark and powerful work, with disturbing metaphysical overtones. Ben Ehrenreich is a gathering power in the literary land." — John Banville, author of *The Infinities* and *The Sea*

"Ben Ehenreich transforms the brutal human and urban blight into a landscape of cosmic battle. *Ether* is a dark, complex, richly written, beautiful novel. It is a rarity in American fiction today." — Frederic Tuten author of *Self Portraits: Fictions* and *Tintin in the New World*

"Ether, perhaps even more than his previous novel, *The Suitors*, shows Ben Ehrenreich unafraid of storytelling that is terrifically bold and sly. Ehrenreich seems to have returned from hiking the ruined wastelands and margins of Port-au-Prince and New Orleans, Mexico City and Los Angeles, Arizona and Phnom Penh, having cracked open the hard nut of the world. Or perhaps Ehrenreich himself has cracked, allowing him to tell this wild, eerie tale of forgiveness for blasted, shattered times. Cries of seabirds from the Gulf of Mexico and pale forms of dying dolphins and porpoises glimmer darkly through it. But in *Ether*, the heart opens and shines a light, magnetic and acrid, smudged and infrared." — Sesshu Foster, author of *World Ball Notebook* and *Atomik Aztex*

ETHER

ETHER

BEN EHRENREICH

City Lights Books • San Francisco

Library of Congress Cataloging-in-Publication Data

Ehrenreich, Ben.
  Ether / Ben Ehrenreich.
    p. cm.
  ISBN 978-0-87286-518-1
  I. Title.
  PS3605.H738E84 2011
  813'.6—dc23
                                    2011029377

City Lights Books are published at the City Lights Bookstore
261 Columbus Avenue, San Francisco, CA 94133
www.citylights.com

for Oso

Would that I knew how to reach Him,
How to get to His dwelling place.
I would set my case before Him,
And fill my mouth with arguments.

Job 23:3-4

Whenever I searched for myself I found
the others. Whenever I searched for the others I found
only my stranger self in them,
so am I the one, the multitude?

Mahmoud Darwish, "Mural"

ONE

The stars.

The sun had long ago set. There was no moon, and the earth was dark. Yet the sky was thick with stars. It was thick too with clouds. The stars circled above them and reeled about the sky. Their light though, for all its will and whimsy, was too weak to be seen from beneath.

The woods also were dark, and the dry fields. Tall yellow lamps lit the highway every fifty yards. From above it looked like nothing more than a long bare necklace of sulfured bulbs, too straight and regular for any constellation. From below it looked like a highway, yellow-tinged. An empty, two-lane, late-night highway. Every third or fourth streetlamp was dark, its bulb shot out by an air gun or a slingshot. There the world was dim. Stars are not so easily extinguished.

But even there, the world was bright with smell and sound — the harsh, dusty smell of the blacktop, the sour mulchy odor of beer cans rotting in the woods, and every now and then the drunk sweetness of datura flowers hanging in trumpets unseen in the dark. Even in the utmost gloom, the world was blinding bright. If you listened, you could hear the wind blow in sudden and uneven fits. Leaves shivered and the dry grass swayed. A crumpled envelope raced across the asphalt. A plastic bag escaped from the low scrub that had ensnared it, leapt free into the breeze but was just as soon caught by a leaning thistle. It jerked and snapped in protest. Beneath it a cricket's forewings sang in expectation. Beetles clacked their jaws. Weevils crunched away at wood. Blood thumped in a bullfrog's brain. Bats winged between the trees. In the dark as in the light, the whole world ate, and hoped to mate.

Spiders snared flies, which ceased to buzz. Owls tore at the hearts of field mice, which ceased to peep. High in a tree and without a sound, a snake swallowed a pale blue egg before it could hatch into a bird. The spider, the owl, the snake — they all delighted. Living things delight in life. Most of them do. Cells divide, and divide again. We mate that our offspring may mate, and eat that our children may eat. So we're told. Blood enriches the soil. The stars shine on above the clouds. This is not an excuse for anyone.

Not for me and least of all for the stranger who walked beneath the yellow streetlamps beneath those clouds beneath the stars, his feet falling one after the other on the gravel at the side of the road. One foot crushed a colony of ants, but he did not appear to notice. The other foot kicked the muddied brown neck of a beer bottle from his path. Mosquitoes bit at his ankles, but he did not slap them away.

His feet stamped on, rising and falling past trees and the stumps of trees, past a discarded refrigerator laid out on its back, its doors hanging open like the wings of some narcoleptic angel, a family of possums breeding in its belly. His feet trudged on past a stray tricycle, past a fire station with windows boarded, no flag on its pole. They didn't pause, didn't slow when he passed a silent clapboard shack and didn't quicken when a dog ran out from behind the shack to howl at him, ears flapping and tail on point. He walked past that dog and past the shadow of a cat a few yards farther down. In another house the lights shone with stubborn joy. Music and laughter leaked out through a broken screen. He kept walking, and did not whistle or mutter or hum. No one marked his passage. Not a single car drove by.

He passed sparse rows of darkened houses followed by stretches a half mile long of waste and woods. The houses leaned against the wind. Dreams circled inside them. Clocks ticked. Dust settled where it could. Insomniacs gripped their sheets. In other groaning houses, their rooftops straining toward the ground, drunks drank at kitchen tables, big sisters whispered to little sisters beneath the blankets covering them, mice dared to race across living room floors, lovers nestled heads on lovers' shoulders. None troubled themselves to notice the gaunt figure that hiked along outside their homes, to wonder who he was and what he wanted, or where his feet would lead him.

They led him at last to a gravel parking lot a mile from any structure save the one it fronted, a low box of a building with a red neon light glowing in its single blackened window. Three cars shared the lot with a green and rusted dumpster. The door, painted a thick and high-gloss brown, trembled slightly to the rhythm of the music within. The stranger stopped, paused a moment just beyond the neon glow, glared hard at the video camera above the door, and slapped the dust from his ankles. He crossed the lot, grabbed the knob, and stepped into the light.

I clear my throat.

I feel I owe you some kind of explanation. An introduction. A preface or prologue of some sort. We haven't met, and I am, after all, imposing.

I live in a small house on a low hill on a short street in a large city. I don't live alone. A woman lives here with me. You won't get to meet her, but she and I sleep side by side on the same lumpy, queen-size mattress in the bedroom in back. She sleeps on the inside, usually on her side but sometimes on her stomach. I sleep on my back, like a corpse I am told, though I do not cross my arms over my chest. I also sleep poorly, and get up often in the night, so I sleep on the outside. I get up and empty my bladder and fill it again with water. Or with whiskey if it's that kind of night. Which tonight it is. I stand barefoot in the kitchen on the cold linoleum until the glass is empty and my throat warm and I can go back to bed. The floor in the hallway is gritty beneath my feet. It needs sweeping, scrubbing. I'll get to it one day.

I pull back the covers and lie listening to her whistling breath, the pace and pitch of it shifting with her dreams. I close my eyes and squeeze them until I see stars. Not really stars, but you know what I mean, as close a substitute as I can hope for. Then I open my eyes and the stars go away. Over the years, we've decorated the walls with posters and photos and prints (Is this straight? Raise the right corner just a smidge. A little lower. There.), but each night the shadows erase all our choices and remake the room according to their own penumbral whims. With the help of the moon, the streetlamps, the headlights and brake lights of each car that drives by, and the on-and-off-again red pinprick light of the video camera mounted in the corner of the ceiling, the shadows keep at it all night long. I lie awake and watch them playing, shifting and stretching, hiding and revealing, changing shape and color, chasing one another from wall to wall.

I can't see them, but I know there are stars above my roof, real ones, up there above the pebbled stucco ceiling and the dark attic I've never crawled inside and the crumbling roof tiles and the overhanging trees and telephone wires and the clouds above them. And there are more stars above those. I count on that, even if the ceiling and the roof and the clouds and the smog and the lights of the city mean that I can rarely see more than one or two of them. They were here before me, the stars, and they'll be here after me, and on nights like this one that's a comfort. But those other stars you read about just now, that mute sky, those woods and fields and sulfured bulbs, the bull-frog and the bats — I built them. Or at least I named them, which amounts to the same thing. I wrote their names, and called them into being. Quite a trick. That street, that sky, this page too and the white between these words, I made them for you. And for myself, because I am selfish, and because I am try-ing to make sense of things.

Forgive me if I'm too abstract, but I am struggling with a conundrum. That conundrum is this world. What is in it. What is not. Mainly what is not. And in that absence — in the knot, if you will, of what is not — what to do with what there is. How to look upon it so that it is not entirely painful. I'll be more specific later. I'll try to anyway, because without you these pages are just pulp, but with you they might begin to form, if not an answer, at least a statement of the problem. An alternate phrasing of the conundrum itself. And that, I hope, might be the beginning of a way out. Better put, of a way in. A way through. For me at least, and perhaps for you as well.

You'll forgive me if I don't start at the beginning. That was too long ago, and hard to pin down. We don't have time. I don't anyway. Besides, taking the long view, nothing really begins, just like nothing ever ends. The cosmos a snake with its tail in its throat, or a turtle sitting atop a turtle, and turtles all the way down. But I have to start somewhere, so it might as well be here, on the hard, slow shell of this old turtle and no other, on this night in particular, here beneath the clouds beneath the dancing stars not in my bedroom anymore but in this gravel parking lot. Wind blowing, trees whispering to trees. A camera humming as it watches from its perch above the door. We left him in mid-stride, his long fingers curled around the doorknob, twisting to the left and to the right, tugging that cold, bronze knob toward him, lifting one foot and then the other, and stepping inside the bar.

He is foiled.

He was tall, with the kind of face you look at once and don't forget, and eyes that burn right through you. His flesh was unlined by age, but his beard was gray and his long and matted hair the same color, perhaps a few shades yellower. He wore a tattered suit that looked to have once been white, but had been spattered, no, crusted, with stains of nearly every color, though mostly a sort of rusted brown. The stains barely showed in the neon dim.

The jukebox in the corner spouted brittle, optimistic pop music, but the bar was nearly empty. A few abandoned balls littered the torn felt of the pool table and like them, the few people in the bar stuck to their positions, intent, apparently, on ignoring one another. The bartender crouched on a stool at the end of the bar, studying the comic book folded on his knees. A man in a John Deere cap snored across from him, the hairs of his long mustache swaying in a puddle of beer with each whistled exhalation. A fat woman in a mini-skirt hugged the jukebox and bobbed with eyes closed to the beat of a song other than the one that the machine was playing. A bald man with no eyebrows and a slight trace of eyeliner conversed intently with an ashtray. "No," the bald man said. "Fuck if I know."

The stranger took a stool near the door beside a slender woman with weathered skin and busy, drink-blurred eyes. She jumped a bit when he sat down. Hooking a lock of hair behind one ear, she bit her lip and then released it into a bright, scared smile. The stranger ordered a Coca Cola. The woman beside him slid a cigarette out of the pack on the bar in front of her.

She looked his way, then consulted the palm of her hand as if hoping to find her lines cribbed there. She tapped her painted nails on the bar, took a deep breath, and spoke. "Got a light?"

The stranger nodded toward the plastic lighter that sat beside her cigarettes. "Oh," she said. "How silly. Silly me."

The woman pushed her hair from her eyes and scratched at the bridge of her nose with her thumb and forefinger. "My name's Marty," she said, and extended a pale, long-fingered hand for him to shake. Her voice, for all its quivering, was as sunny as anything could be in the heavy gloom of the bar. "It's Martha, really, but nobody calls me that 'cept my mom when she's not calling me something nasty."

She giggled, embarrassed. He took her hand and nodded, but said nothing in return.

Marty sucked on her cigarette and blew a wide cone of smoke from one corner of her mouth. She scratched her nose and tried again. "You're not from around here," she said. "Are you?"

The stranger sipped at his cola. "I am," he said, smiling tightly. "From here. Here and pretty much everywhere."

"You must've been here way back then, cause I never seen you, and I know just about everyone."

Marty laughed. Together they listened to her laughter fade and fall before he spoke. The ice in his soda crackled as it melted.

"Yes," he said. "Way back."

Marty took a short breath and, already blushing, gave his knee a light, experimental slap with the back of her hand. "Wash you up a little and you'd be cute as a kitten," she beamed. "You got those matinee eyes."

He twisted his beard into one long thin braid, looked up

at her from beneath bushy white eyebrows, and returned her smile.

She stared at her lap. She suddenly looked very tired, as if the gloom of the bar had seeped beneath her defenses, extinguishing what little cheer she had struggled to ignite. Her voice was thin and weak when she spoke again. "You gonna ask me if you can buy me a drink?"

He asked, and she consented. He paid with crumpled bills, and tipped the bartender with a handful of change. Her drink arrived in a tall, fluted glass, with a wedge of orange and a pink paper umbrella on its rim. She emptied it in three long gulps, sucked the orange from its rind, and wiped her mouth on her wrist. The drink seemed to revive her. "I'll tell you," she said, twirling the umbrella between her thumb and forefinger, "You're lucky you got outta this town, cause it is dead." She spelled it. "D-E-A-D, dead."

He smiled again, more warmly this time. "Looks like there's a little life in it yet."

"I try," she said, her eyebrows raised. "Lord knows I try."

"Lord knows," he agreed.

Marty stared at the bottles arrayed in tiers behind the bar. She did not take her eyes from them until she finished talking. "I quit my job today," she began, blinking at the recollection. "That's why I'm here. Celebrating. If you couldn't tell. I don't know why I quit it, but I did. Sometimes you need a change. That's what I told myself. Funny thing is though, it was the best job I ever had. Really. Good pay, the boss was nice enough. Or almost nice. I liked the other people, some of them. It was fine. But I woke up this morning and I could not bear to go in. I just couldn't. So I went back to sleep and when the phone rang I told him I quit. That's it, I just quit. Then I came here. Sometimes you need a change."

Marty hugged herself for a moment. She scratched again at her nose and lifted her glass to her lips. There was nothing in it but ice. "My mother died," she said, her voice barely a whisper. "Yesterday."

The stranger offered no response.

She fumbled in her purse and came out with a small chromed plastic tube. She lit another cigarette and, between puffs, applied the lipstick to her lips. Narrowing her eyes, she considered the figure perched beside her. "You believe in god?" she asked.

"Believe?"

"Yeah, believe. Is that a personal question? Cause every time I ask someone that I feel like it's a personal question, like I just asked for your bank statements or if you like sniffing panties. Can I just ask you that? Is that too much?"

"You can ask."

"Good. Cause sometimes I don't want to talk about the weather, or the lottery, or whatever. How cute my dog is. Sometimes . . ." She didn't finish the thought, but took one last drag from her cigarette and sat while it smoldered to the filter in the ashtray. "It wasn't my mother that died," she said. "It was my little girl." She covered her face with her hands.

She did not sob, just quivered slightly. The stranger made no attempt to console her. He stared without expression at his own reflected image among the bottles in the mirror across the bar. The song on the jukebox faded out. Silence spread to the corners of the barroom like an angry, buzzing haze. You could hear, or almost hear, or could imagine you could hear, the camera above the pool table swiveling on its mount. The fat woman who had been dancing alone stopped dancing, but not until a minute or so after the music had ceased to play. With a jangle of keys and a muttered "That's it then," she stumbled to the door.

Marty lifted her face from her hands. Her eyes were red, but they were dry, and her cheeks were not streaked with tears. "Don't worry," she said. "Nobody died." She shook the ice in her glass. "Everything's just fine." She swiveled towards him on her stool and flashed a quick, sad smile. She put a hand on his knee, then pulled it back again.

He turned to her and spoke. "Do you?" he asked.

"Do I what?" she said.

"Do you believe? In god?

She knit her brow. "That's nice of you to ask," she said, "but it's really none of your fucking business." Then Marty laughed a high and wheezy laugh, winked, and took his hand in hers. "I'm joking, sweetheart. You can ask me anything you want."

The stranger pulled his hand away. She whispered hurriedly in his ear. "Listen, you like blow? Cause I got some in my bag."

Without waiting for a response, she grabbed him by his thumb and led him to the back of the bar and through a door labeled "Gals." She locked the feeble hook and eye behind him. As she rummaged through her bag, facing the sink and looking up at him every few seconds in the soap-stained mirror as if it were necessary to reassure herself that he had not already disappeared, she reached one palm behind her and rested it shakily on his chest. Her hand dropped down and gripped his belt. He took a single step back.

"Don't let me scare you," she said, locating at last in the cluttered depths of her purse a small pocket mirror and a plasticine bag of clumpy white powder. She laughed weakly. "I scare all the good ones away." She turned around to face him. "Only the bad ones stick around," she said. "And the worse ones."

She tapped the powder onto the glass of the mirror, crushing any pebbled bits with the edge of her drivers license and cutting the resulting pile into four short lines. "Got a bill?" she said.

He pulled one from his pocket, crumpled like the others.

"That won't work." She produced a crisp twenty of her own, rolled it into a thin straw and sucked one line into each of her nostrils before offering him the mirror. He shook his head.

"You don't want?" The surprise in her eyes fell away swiftly. "Why'd you come in here," she asked with a coy grin, "if you don't want?"

Marty flushed at her own forwardness, cocked her head back and snorted. She squeezed shut her eyes as the drug sped from synapse to synapse. She shivered. "You're gonna be nice to me, aren't you?"

She didn't wait for an answer, but lowered her head to sniff the remaining lines. Before she could, he shot out an arm and took her by the throat with his hand. Her pocket mirror bounced on the linoleum. White powder dusted her boots. He began to squeeze. She jammed her knee into his scrotum and when he doubled over, she caught him beneath the chin with an uppercut that sent him sprawling onto the toilet behind him.

"Fucking freak!" she yelled, then grabbed her purse, spat in his face, and slammed the door behind her.

The stranger stood, straightened his jacket and his pants

and splashed his face with water from the sink. It was brown, and the sink was clogged with cigarette butts, what looked to be a tampon. From behind the door, he could hear the woman yelling. "That fucking fucker tried to fucking kill me," she shrieked. A second or two later, the door swung open and a white light shattered between his temples. When he came to, the barkeep was carrying him out, gripping him by the back of the neck. His feet dragged behind him like a doll's. The barkeep opened the door and tossed him into the parking lot.

He lifted himself onto his elbows. His eyes shone with rage. "Damn you," he hissed. "Damn you to hell."

Standing in the doorway, the bartender laughed. "Shit," he said. "That's a good one." And with that he spat a full tablespoon of tobacco juice onto what was left of the stranger's white suit, and closed the door behind him.

The bird.

In the darkened streets she made her rounds. The night was cool, the streets quiet. But it was not the heat and certainly not the noise that kept the woman awake. She could neither hear nor speak, and some nights she also could not sleep. Some nights, and some days too, swarms of sharp-winged flies invaded her skull, entering through her ears and nose and through the corners of her mouth and circling madly in the small black-orange room between her forehead and the rear wall of her cranium. The only thing to do was walk, so she gathered her skirts about her and climbed the embankment into the streets.

The night felt safer than the day. Darkness, the woman knew, has its privileges. Blindness too, and even deafness. At night there were no cars to hit her on the avenues, no looming trucks, no people to scold her for one or another imagined sin. There were fewer men to pull her into alleys, no bored policemen choosing their targets from behind mirrored shades, no sneakered women with clipboards and government name tags, lips pursed in pity but eyes dead to care. She had no fear of rats and the dogs left her alone.

She crouched to pass through a hole in the fence and cross from the concrete lip of the embankment through the tangled weeds to the lots between the warehouses. She walked down the middle of the potholed street. Searching the walls for cameras, she saw none. Steel shutters had been pulled closed over the loading bays. Even the high windows of the warehouses had been painted black or gray. At night the buildings had no eyes. Their mouths were sewn shut. This was a comfort to her — to pass unseen, unspoken to — and also, of course, a torment. Invisibility has its costs. If no one saw her, she asked herself, was she even there?

But the woman was not entirely alone. It hardly counts as company, but she soon came across a man. She almost stumbled over him where he lay curled on the ground beside a dumpster. His eyes were closed, his mouth open. In lieu of a blanket, he wore a lumpy army-surplus jacket. He wheezed in short, troubled breaths, hugging an empty bottle like an infant to his breast. She tiptoed around him — wary, keeping her feet and ankles at least an arm's length from his sleep-twitching hands — and lifted the corner of the dumpster's lid. It was empty save a cardboard box, which was also empty, so she rushed away and did not slow until she had put a block between them. Only once she had gazed back and seen the shadow of him there unmoving, like a lump in the pitted asphalt, did she allow herself to pause and pull a stone from her shoe.

A block away, she stopped again and watched the insects circling in the inverted funnels of yellow light that hung down from the streetlamps to her right and to her left. She tried to count them but soon gave up. There were too many and they flickered about too quickly. Some of them were moths. All of them spiraled expectantly upward, abandoning for this one bright chance at transcendence all the screaming demands of sustenance and procreation. Who can blame them? A bat flitted from lamp to lamp and picked them off.

She clanked open the lids of the dumpsters in the alley beside a produce warehouse and found a full crate of pears wedged among the bulbous trash bags. The fruits were too ripe and too bruised to sell, but not to eat. She heaved out the crate and laid it in the shadows at the edge of the alley where she could find it again on her way back. She took one pear with her, biting through its browning flesh. The juice ran down her chin and onto her chest through the open collars of her shirts. She smiled at its sweetness, chewing as she walked.

The woman passed a sprawling cinderblock building indistinguishable from the rest but which she knew to be a distribution hub for plastic toys, a sort of vast nursery and holding pen for injection-molded infants, ponies, soldiers and bears. She ducked to dodge a swiveling camera, climbed a fence and tried the dumpsters. Two were locked, one was empty and a fourth was filled only with pink plastic shavings, shredded paper and the crusted styrofoam remains of workers' meals — no dolls or parts of dolls.

Around the corner, on the other side of the now-sleepy highway, behind the wholesale flower mart, she found a mound of discarded bouquets of the most extraordinary blossoms: petals like meteors, like velvet curtains, like bayonets; pistils like furred stag's legs, like spotted towers, stigmata that looked soft and wide enough to sleep on. Their stems had broken, so the florists deemed them ruined. She could carry at least two bouquets, she figured, stacked atop the pears. As she knelt to choose among them, she saw to her surprise that one of the flowers was twitching. It was a huge, drooping, pudendal bloom, red, yellow and black and pulsing furiously as if wired to a miniature engine. She lifted it, and the flower fell still. On the pavement beneath, she found a tiny bird. It was a hummingbird, no bigger than her thumb. One of its wings lay outstretched beneath it like another strange petal. Its other wing beat with such speed that she could barely see it. For all its effort, the bird could not fly.

She scooped the bird up with her fingers and folded its broken wing against its tiny, humming body. It weighed less than the flower that had covered it. In her hand, the hummingbird was still. The wing ceased its fluttering. Its shiny, black, pinprick of an eye did not express pain or panic or anything at all. But even in the dull, sepia light of the streetlamp, the bird's plumage shimmered from green to red to gold and seemed to be all of those colors at once. She stroked its head with the pad of her index finger and placed it gently in the breast pocket of her outermost shirt. She picked two bouquets of flowers and went back to fetch the fruit.

Walking home, she stopped every few paces, set down her load and lifted the bird from her pocket. Its heart whirred like a turbine in her palm.

He dials an old friend.

The stranger limped down the highway in the dark. After a few miles of rutted asphalt he came across a gas station. It was closed and deserted but for the mosquitoes that circled in the flickering light above the pumps. He fed a pocketful of nickels into the pay phone in the corner of the parking lot, beside the ice machine. He let it ring fourteen times before he hung up. The nickels clanged down again and bounced rolling to the blacktop. He sat on the ground among them and leaned his back against the post on which the phone was hung. Above the phone, a camera blinked red. He slept for half an hour without snoring, his face untroubled by dreams. Then he tried again, depositing nickel after nickel into the coin slot until at last the phone began to ring. Fourteen more rings passed, then fourteen more. At last a hoarse voice answered. He asked for Gabriel.

"He's asleep."

"So wake him." He heard silence, then a click. He dug around for more nickels, dialed again.

"What," the hoarse voice growled.

"Gabriel," he said. "Wake him. I'll make it worth your while."

There was a pause. "And who the fuck are you?"

"Take a chance. Believe me. Good will come your way. Do this one thing for me."

"He gets up early, around six." Again, a click, then a dial tone. The stranger crouched on the asphalt again, and slept beneath the phone until the sun rose. This time he slept uneasily, his body shaking, his fists clenched, shadows of dreams chasing themselves across his face.

As soon as he woke he called again. The desk clerk made him wait while he sent up to Gabriel's room, and he had to feed the phone once more with coins. At last Gabriel picked up. "Gabriel," he said. "It's me."

Gabriel said nothing for a long while. "Why are you calling me?" he finally said.

"I need a favor, Gabriel."

"Try someone else. I'm all out."

"Just one last time. For old time's sake."

"Forget it."

"Thank you, Gabriel. I really mean that. I'll be there tomorrow. I won't forget this."

"I said forget it," Gabriel said. "It's over." He hung up. The stranger hung up too, smiled to himself, and started off down the road.

The problem with things.

Things were in crisis. The sun still shone. Daily it rose. Daily it set. The moon worked its circuit and also the stars. If you squinted your eyes, everything seemed all right. But things did not fit themselves. Though they continued to function as if nothing had changed. That was the worst of it. The bagman did not know how else to put it except that things no longer appeared to be contained by their own outlines. Ordinary things. Sidewalks, cars, what have you. They seemed too tight, too baggy, ill-meshed to one another, all bunched up. They sat wrong with themselves. The textures seemed false, the smells manufactured. The colors were off. Things appeared to mock themselves. Every single thing seemed an imperfect parody of its own essence.

It had not always been so. The bagman had not always been a bagman. That much he was able to acknowledge. He'd had a name once, though he no longer cared to recollect it. He had been a citizen of the most ordinary sort, an unquestioning believer in the thingness of things, in their coherence and singularity. He had shopped in shopping malls, gone to bed in a bedroom, dined, at times, in diners. He had worn ordinary clothes and smelled of ordinary soap. Pressed khakis. V-neck sweaters. Dove. Prell. But his life had been cleaved by an incident that he was only willing to let himself think of — and then cautiously, as if handling a bare wire that might be live, with steel pliers and wet hands — as The Incident. And the only thing that you or I will get to know about The Incident is that it happened, that it was done. Those two words contained for the bagman all the uncontainable enormity of the past tense. He used them to construct a shade with which to cover from view the actual event and the chain of events that followed it — the infinite, incomprehensible connections between them, the mute stupidity of time — a shade that served to hide all but the fuzziest contours of the bagman's pre-bag life. What had been, the bagman knew, no longer was. The Incident, like the astral phenomenon inaccurately called a black hole, sucked all he knew inside it and stranded him alone in the world, hollow and hungry, a bearded, malodorous, birth-defected newborn, lost and already slightly broken. Around the edges of that hole that was not a hole, the bagman felt a deep, thirsting anxiety, and something akin to guilt.

In better moods, he tried to laugh. He rarely drank, but when he did he found it easier. And by it, I mean, well, all of it. He could pretend it was a joke and that he was in on the joke. Pick up a pint of Karlov from the Korean man behind the plexiglass cage at the corner store, sip on a park bench, scratch his big, grey belly and toast the world, wink wink. Toast the squirrels and the ants and the cameras hidden in the trees and the weeds that grew in the cracks in the cement, widening the cracks, turning cement to sand, to dust. Toast the clouds and the wind and the birds that swam squawking from tree branch to tree branch, and the squawks that lingered in the pulsing space between the branches. Raise the bottle to the smell of jasmine in the springtime, the first-rain smell of fall, the smell of urine all year long. Toast the clicking of heels on the sidewalk, the hum of passing cars outside the park, the muttering and whispering of the men and women who had sat here yesterday and all the days before that, a child's voice somewhere behind him, the child's ball as it escaped the child's hands and bounced away down the concrete path

But the joviality was hard to sustain. There were too many things. They stared him down. Vodka can only get you so far. Invariably, it would cause him to fall asleep, a not so unpleasant outcome if it were not that he always eventually woke, and usually at some middle level of despair. Not quite the bottom floor — to which he felt no desire to return — but still much too near the basement. Mouth dry, head throbbing with questions: even if it was a joke, whose joke was it? More important, on whom? And joke or calamity, if a thing was no longer itself, if its skin had been somehow stretched or shrunk and altered, what was it? What was anything in this mad, sick blur? Could he rest his weight on this earth and know that it would bear him?

These questions, of course, do not pertain solely to the bagman. I don't mind admitting that they're mine as well — how else could I have known to write them, to attribute them to him? But the bagman, limited as he was by the four rounded corners of his skull, had no way of knowing this and tried on occasion to check in with others, to determine if he was alone in his concerns. He was not successful. Other people, he found, did not wish to speak with him. Approached, they scurried from him with mouths clamped shut. As if he were something contagious. (His code of dress, it should be said, did not conform to prevailing social norms. Nor, perhaps more crucially, did his approach to hygiene.) And even if people had stopped to listen, had opened themselves to him fully, the truth was that words fought him with even greater avidity than stone-mute things. They flitted between his ears like drunken moths, turning to vapor before he could force them through his mouth. If it cost him a near-Herculean effort to construct and impart the simplest declarative proposition, what hope could he have to convey such vast and metaphysical quandaries?

Nonetheless, he gathered evidence. He hoped for a tribunal, a chance to make his case. Before whom, he wasn't sure. Nor against whom. He planned to collect one of everything. That was his original intent. To make a comprehensive case. To be able to display at least one instance of every single thing, like Noah if Noah had herded all the beasts in the world up the gangplank and onto the ark for purposes of prosecution rather than preservation. As evidence. He was limited by finances, of which he had none. This restricted him to things found abandoned or which he could handily nick. And to things small enough to carry, as he had no secure abode of his own in which to store them.

Isn't this counterintuitive? Wouldn't he be moved to flee the things that menaced him, and not to hug them to him? Well it's hard to get away from things. Even in sleep, even in stupor, there they are, stubborn as your shadow. And the bagman, as you shall see, was a man of considerable courage. He dodged the past (if *dodge* is the right word for his careful self-immurement), but he flinched at nothing else. He ran bravely forward, if never back. He handled each of the objects he harvested as an exterminator treats a rat he's caught alive, with a thick admixture of revulsion, curiosity, and affection bred by bondage to a task.

He laid up his gleanings in big plastic trash bags and carried them with him everywhere. He filled one bag and then another. Three he could carry, but for more than that he needed a cart. Something existed in the makeup of police officers, he had learned, some broken neural switch, frayed fascicles perhaps, or a congenitally torn meninx: they did not like to see a man push a cart. Their reactions were unpredictable and tended toward extremes. It didn't matter. He quickly found that there was insufficient regularity even among things of any given category — socks, for instance, or rubber bands — to justify his original ambition. He could argue his case just as effectively if his body of evidence consisted entirely of rubber bands, every rubber band being distinct from every other rubber band and all of them, every single one, failing in some inchoate but nonetheless essential manner to actually *be* a rubber band. So he culled his collection and left the cart in an alley.

To save his back the trouble of hauling inessential weight, he confined himself to objects he deemed especially illustrative of the general crisis. These objects were not necessarily deformed or damaged in any describable fashion, though many were. Some were new and spotless exemplars of their type, still shrink-wrapped even, and it was as such that he chose them, if only to prove that, as an uncle had told him many forgotten years before, you can't spitshine a turd.

It did occur to him with nagging persistence that the root of the problem might lie closer to home, that the collected artifacts of creation were as they'd always been, but *he* had somehow slipped his boundaries. It could be, he realized, a problem of perception, though his eyes, at least, were fine. He decided not to pursue that possibility. It led him with excruciating inevitability to the high and crenellated parapets encircling The Incident, and to a painful question: if he could muster no faith in the world or in any of the myriad things that comprise it, what right had he to walk among them?

But this would get him nowhere. Perhaps, he decided, it was simply a question of context. Perhaps things were just in disarray, not damned each and every one. And if things — not all things, but the limited series of objects in his personal possession — could be arranged in the proper order, like puzzle pieces, or magic words, or the digits of a pass-code, everything might again become itself. And he might rest.

He pays a visit.

Gabriel lived on the fourth floor of the Redemption Arms Hotel. The sign in the lobby read, "No Guests, No Exceptions," but they sneaked past the desk when the clerk was in the john. Gabriel's room was an eight-foot-by-eight-foot square of graffiti-scarred plaster, once painted beige but now various shades of brown and yellow and even blue from the grease from people's hair, their saliva and other excretions, particles of food. The walls only went up about seven feet, and the remaining space between the sheetrock and the ceiling was filled with a single length of chicken wire, which made it feel as much like a cage as a room. Between the exposed and cobweb-coated beams of the ceiling was a dust-smudged mirrored dome concealing cameras, or at least suggesting the possibility of such concealment. But whether the dome above was empty or filled with watchful electronic eyes did not matter. Everything said and done in every room could be heard in every other. They sat on Gabriel's bed and listened to muzzled sounds of fucking rise from one room, unmuzzled weeping from another, and somewhere a cheery pop melody leaking thinly from the speaker of a transistor radio.

Gabriel sipped at a warm quart of Miller High Life. "I wish I could say it was good to see you," he said. His hands were shaking.

"C'mon, Gabriel," the stranger said. "Why all the bitterness?"

Gabriel just snorted. "Funny," he said. He pushed an oiled strand of hair from his brow. "You're funny."

The stranger leaned back to better regard his friend, who

wore heavy black-framed glasses taped in one corner with duct tape, faded jeans and a t-shirt that depicted an enormous hand, index finger extended to one side, and the words "I'm with stupid." Gabriel was unhsaven. Broken blood vessels lined his cheeks. The stranger beheld all this — the bloat of Gabriel's eyes, his thinning hair — and spoke. "You look good. You do."

"Yeah, I'm a looker. You look like shit. What happened to your suit?"

The stranger smiled and shook his head. He held one hand cupped inside the other. "I'll be honest," he said. "Things aren't what they used to be."

"They never were."

The stranger nodded. "Maybe not. I made mistakes. I'll be the first to admit it. I was short-sighted. I was immodest."

Gabriel laughed.

"Is that funny?" the stranger asked. "I'm trying to be straight with you. Give me a little credit here. I was headstrong. I was proud. I know that. Look at me now. Look at this fucking suit, Gabriel. I'm in rags. Me. Rags. Like a stinking Bowery bum. How could I not know I made mistakes? And still you hate me."

Gabriel fished a cigarette butt from the ashtray on the dresser. "Yes," he said. He lit the butt and shook out the match.

"You have every right."

"I know."

They were silent, Gabriel standing by the dresser, hands on his hips, smoke rising from his cigarette like a curtain across his face. His guest sat on the unmade bed, on the gray sheets, his shoulders hunched. He stared at his knees and in a whisper said, "I'm sorry." A few rooms over the moaning rose to a crescendo. "Please, baby," someone said, panting. "Please." There was a shriek of pleasure, then a grunt, then a voice again, softer now, thick-throated: "Baby, please."

Gabriel ashed on the floor. "What do you want?" he asked.

"I need your help," the stranger said. "I need a favor."

"What?"

"I want to set things right."

"You're too late."

"Please, Gabriel. I'm asking you. Help me."

"What about Michael? Ask him."

"He's in law school. Just bought himself a Saab. Married. Useless."

A smile crossed Gabriel's lips and just as quickly fled. He lifted the beer to his mouth. He said it again, more a statement than a question. "What do you want."

"I want to be back on top. I can't fix it unless I can get back up. I want to undo the damage, to do it again but right."

Gabriel shook his head. "You don't learn," he said.

"I do learn. I have learned. That's why I'm here. That's why I'm humbling myself before you Gabriel."

"What do you want from me."

The stranger straightened his back, raised his eyes, caught Gabriel's eyes in his. "Be my sword," he said, then whispered it again. "Be my sword."

Whole volumes of text skittered across Gabriel's face: epic narratives of temptation, disgust, regret. Then whatever bright conglomeration of emotion animating them was extinguished, and his eyes went blank, dull, dead. Gabriel spat a fleck of tobacco onto the floor. "It's over," he said. "No more."

His visitor rose from the bed. "I won't ask again," he said.

Gabriel dropped his eyes. He picked at a scab on his knuckle. He scratched behind his ear. "Good," he said.

A wide, warm smile stretched across the stranger's face. He tossed a few crumpled bills at Gabriel's pillow. "Buy yourself a bender," he said. "Enjoy your life. I've taken too much of your time already, Gabriel, you have things to do, I'm sure. But it's been good to catch up. Really. Now, before I go, I must ask you to give me something, something of mine that you will no longer need."

Gabriel shrugged. "It's under the bed," he said.

I lie awake.

I lie awake and listen to the helicopter drone overhead. The police up there as always, a loud and clumsy eye watching over everything, or trying to, skimming above the gridded streets, squinting, spying, bloodrimmed. The searchlight licks at the curtains. It comes into our room. It is brazen enough to reach in through the open window and caress her ankle while I lie on the bed beside her. She doesn't stir. The light withdraws. The helicopter flies away, and circles back, and flies away again.

It was her cries that woke me. Or maybe before she cried out, when her body first tensed and her hand dropped from my hip so that she could hug herself and fend off whatever dreamtime demon was attacking. I tried to wake her, my hands on her shoulders. It's okay baby wake up baby it's okay. But she whimpered and shook and dodged behind her hands. It's okay baby I'm here wake up. She didn't wake. The whimpers turned to sobs, fear to grief and still under the cover of sleep. I stroked her hair and kissed her forehead and her twitching eyelids until another dream overtook the first and she slept there in the crook of my arm. I couldn't see her dreams. I tried but I could not see them. And if I couldn't then how could I possibly help? So I listened to the trucks clank by out on the avenue. For a while I watched the ceiling fan. It did not do anything unusual. The camera above the bed blinked red. A dog barked. Somewhere a rooster crowed. The helicopter circled over someone else's house.

I ease my arm out from under her. I touch her cheek and watch her sleep. Her hair spills across the pillows. Her breasts rising, catching, falling. A tiny moan. She turns on her side, away from me. She curls into herself. I sip at the water on the table beside the bed. I stand and shut the door behind me. I shuffle out to the porch, and sit, and wish I still smoked cigarettes. Perhaps I wouldn't have been moved to write this if I still smoked, or if I drank the way I used to. But my lungs are shot and barstools bore me now, so I try to sit still. My feet are cold. I listen for crickets and coyotes, but I hear none. I see no moon, no stars, no shooting stars. The wind is silent. The helicopter's gone. The streets are empty, frozen, lined on both sides with sleeping cars. The streetlamps reflect off the clouds and off each other. What can I do but write to you?

This is the world. I need to see it clearly. These empty streets and all they hold. The stranger who pads through my dreams. Or who would if I could sleep, if I had dreams. But even here, on this dim porch, more awake than I want to be, I smell his tattered suit, the tired grease of him. I want you to see him too, wherever it is that you are reading this. On a train perhaps. On a sofa with your feet up. At your desk, pretending to work. On a hard, backless bench, waiting for the bus. In bed, beside someone or alone with the sheets. Did I guess right? It doesn't matter. I want you to see him right here where I am, and in this empty street where he cannot be seen, and in the dark and sleepy rooms behind me where he also is not. I want you to see him as I see him, because I need you to see this world, and me in it, alone as you are. That does matter to me, though I can't quite tell you why.

On my porch is a small wooden table, a potted plant, two mismatched wooden chairs. I sit in one. He's in the other. His legs are crossed and he's humming to himself. I can't make out the tune. A streetlamp flickers. A possum scoots across the sidewalk. Somewhere a dog barks. Coyotes answer. Or maybe that's a siren, distorted as it bounces through the hills. The stranger slowly taps one foot. He's calm but hardly patient. He turns to me and speaks. "I have to go," he says.

"Okay," I say. "Then go."

He makes a deal.

The stranger left the hotel with a package tucked beneath the jacket of his suit. It was wrapped in oil-stained brown paper and bound with twine. Its weight made him stoop slightly to one side. The paper crinkled as he walked. After two blocks he flagged a bus, paid the driver and headed for the back, passing women clutching infants to their breasts, students in plaid skirts blushing and giggling, men in faded clothing with headphones on their ears, nodding and sometimes nodding off. The rear of the bus was nearly empty. A sharp smell hung over the aisle, like a soft French cheese aged in soiled tube socks. It did not appear to bother the stranger, who took a seat in the last row and laid the package on his lap. He gripped it with both hands.

Beside him sat the source of the odor, a large man in a knit cap, his beard as white as the stranger's, his eyes as yellow as the two teeth that jutted forth between his blistered lips. The man wore a black woolen sweater with woven reindeer in green and red gallivanting across his chest. The sweater was too small, and revealed the three layers of dun-colored under-shirts he wore beneath it, all of them also too small, so that his grey-brown belly puckered forth bare above the waistband of his sweatpants. Arrayed around the man were his belongings, by which you will likely recognize him: three green lawn and leaf bags stuffed to bursting with fabric — a flannel shirt, a pillowcase, an argyle sock — and with rusted bicycle chains, plastic toys, balls of rubber bands, an empty box of cookies. The bagman hummed to himself as he emptied one of the bags, piling its contents on the seat between him and the stranger, dividing his possessions with great care between the two remaining bags, in turn removing their contents to make room for the new.

The bus's air brakes squealed. Weaving through traffic, it heaved back and forth and from side to side, but the stranger, like the fulcrum of a pendulum, did not shift in his seat. The bagman, swaying with the lunges of the bus, paused in his humming and ceased his rearranging to observe for a moment the still, white-suited man beside him. He fixed his gaze on the paper-wrapped package clutched to the stranger's knees. For a moment, it took his breath away. He almost could not bear to look at it. It was precisely what it was.

He directed his eyes at the front of the bus, somewhere just above the driver's head, but his words were for the stranger. "Trade ya," he said, his voice deep and hollow, echoey.

The stranger turned his head to his left and regarded his neighbor with a cool curiosity. "Trade me what?" he asked.

The man with the bags gazed upward and searched the air above his head. "All of this," he replied, as if biting off each word. "All I got."

"For what?" the stranger asked.

"All you got."

The stranger considered the offer. "You want what I have?"

His interlocutor's yellow eyes returned to the package on his lap. They did not blink. The bagman nodded.

The stranger shook his head. "You cannot have what I have," he said. "But I will take what's yours. All that's yours is mine. Do you understand?"

The bagman thought for a moment, then nodded his assent. "Okay," he said. He stared hard at the tank-topped shoulder of a woman three rows up. He gripped his knees with both hands. "But what do I get?"

"You get to carry it," the stranger said. "You get what you need."

A shiver ran up the bagman's spine and his mouth emitted something less than a moan but far more than an ordinary exhalation. He nodded again. "Deal," he said, and offered forth his hand.

The stranger beheld the hand, its scabbed knuckles and ochrous, filth-caked nails. "Don't ever touch me," he said, and smiled.

The dog.

It started with the dog. The long-haired girl was driving her father's car, just around the neighborhood and not too fast but they were laughing about something (they would never remember what), when the short-haired girl suddenly gripped her by the shoulder and yelled "Stop!" A dog lay in the road. An old dog, its long and probably deaf ears streaked with gray and splayed out on the pavement. The long-haired girl yanked at the wheel and stomped the brake. The car swerved up onto the curb. The short-haired girl slid hard across the wide bench seat, so hard that when the car came to a stop she found that she was lying with her head in her best friend's lap, facing upward with her eyes clamped shut. She opened them and saw the long-haired girl looking down at her, her face frozen in that moment of panicked action. She began to laugh again, harder than before.

"Shit," said the long-haired girl, perturbed. "You should really wear a seat belt." But then she too began to laugh and she put her hand on the upturned cheek of her friend. When they were done laughing her hand was still there. With her finger, the long-haired girl traced the curve of the short-haired girl's mouth, the bow of her lips and the shallow gutter that connected them to her nose. She placed her thumb between her best friend's teeth. Her friend bit down on it. "Ouch," she said.

The short-haired girl sat up on her elbows. Her cheeks were flushed. She reached up and placed one hand behind the head of the long-haired girl. She pulled her closer. But the long-haired girl's seat belt locked and would not let her move.

They giggled, scared this time and barely breathing. The long-haired girl reached around to unbuckle the belt, and bent to kiss her friend.

Their hands were everywhere. They bit each other's ears, and lips, and shoulders. They kissed each other's eyelids and the tips of each other's noses. They told each other jokes composed entirely of kisses that tickled them more than any joke they'd heard before. They sucked at each other's tongues as if they knew that they could find no other sustenance, not ever. They rolled on top of one another and switched places, and switched places again. They found such softness in each other's flesh that they did not imagine could exist in life. They panted, and whimpered softly. The short-haired girl shed five soft ecstatic tears.

When they had finished, the two friends lay for a long while and held each other tight. The long-haired girl rebuttoned the short-haired girl's shorts and leaned forward so that the short-haired girl could zip her skirt for her.

"Did we really just do that?" asked the short-haired girl.

"I don't know," the long-haired girl said. "I don't know what we did." She bit her lip, stifled a smile, and kissed her friend some more.

They sat up. The car straddled the sidewalk, one rear wheel in the street, the two front tires on someone's weedy lawn. A few yards to the right of the short-haired girl's window, the dog snored in the street. Its lip fluttered up, then fell, then shivered up again. They watched the dog sleep, and squeezed each other's hands.

He finds a spot. For resting.

When twelve blocks later the bus shrieked to a halt, the stranger pushed through the doors and stepped onto the pavement. The bus pitched forward a few yards before lurching to a stop again. Its rear doors swung out once more, like an insect's wings, or the opening of a mechanical mouth. First one green plastic bag then a second shot out from between the doors, like eggs or some uncertain offspring of smooth polymeric extrusion. After them, the bagman tumbled out, carrying a third bag in his arms, panting already. He crouched, heaved all three bags over his shoulders and carried them like that, two in his right hand and one in the left. "Hey," he said to the stranger, almost choking from the effort to speak. "Wait up."

But the stranger did not wait. The bagman had to run to keep pace with him. He dropped here one bag, there another, and paused to restuff them with contents spilled out on the sidewalk: a plastic canary, a pair of children's underpants decorated with race cars and locomotives, a broken, keyless calculator. "Hey," the bagman bellowed, jiggling along the sidewalk at full canter, panting to keep up with the stranger's loping stride. "Wait."

This time the stranger stopped. He even turned around. The bagman put down his bags and mopped at his brow with his cap. He straightened his sweater. "There's a spot I know," the bagman said. He shuffled his feet. He stared down at the weeds growing in the cracks of the cement, at flattened disks of chewing gum, at a pigeon pecking at the yellow filter of a discarded cigarette. He pursed his lips and spoke again. "For resting. Cause soon it's dark."

The stranger thought it over. He eyed the bagman hungrily. "A spot you know," he said. "For resting." He nodded. The bagman shouldered his burden and shuffled off, humming to himself, the stranger at his side.

They walked at least a mile through the city streets. They shouldered their way down a busy block of restaurants through cashmered crowds cooing over window-mounted menus. They passed shop windows stacked with flat-screened televisions as wide as bedsheets and mobile telephones smaller than your thumb. They stepped over the legs of sleeping children, curled naked on the concrete beneath t-shirts worn like dresses. They hiked through an empty warehouse district where they watched a single carp leaping and swimming in the rubbishy streams that coursed the gutters. They passed a midget woman with sores on her arms, throat and brow, dancing alone in an alley, her face contorted with anguish, tears tumbling down her cheeks — no music, no moans or sobs or sighs, just grieving ballerina pantomime. The bagman stopped to watch her, but the stranger did not pause and when the bagman noticed he'd been left behind, he reshouldered his bags and hurried after him. In the alley, the woman pliéed and pirouetted, and executed a perfect weeping entrechat.

They crossed acres of railroad yards, kicking through the ballast, hopping the tracks, dodging unmoored boxcars rolling huge and silent beneath the hunched brown sun. They trekked past an abandoned dog track and on through a field of brambles where plastic potato chip bags skipped in the wind. At last they stopped beneath a concrete freeway overpass. Speeding cars breathed loud above them. "Here," the bagman said, and laid down his bags beside a pillar.

From the bottom of the leftmost bag, he fished out a small dust broom and on his knees began to brush away the refuse of other people's pleasures — broken bottles, broken lighters, yellowed cigarette filters, tiny empty ziplock baggies, small glass tubes with colored plastic stoppers — until he had cleared an even quadrangle of pavement about eight feet wide and four feet long.

A mouse scampered by across the far end of this clearing, and despite his age and girth, the bagman leapt two nimble yards through the air and landed with acrobatic grace and one outstretched toe on the squeaking mouse's tail. He lifted the toe. The mouse ran, bulge-eyed and blind, and collided with the bagman's other foot, with which he stomped the creature dead. It barely crunched. He tossed it by its tail into the scrub, splashing the concrete with a trail of small red droplets.

The stranger grinned. "Bravo," he said, and clapped three times.

The bagman grunted and went on sweeping, striating the mouse's clotting blood along the pavement, mixing it with the mineral dust of the earth, the fine black ash spat from the exhaust pipes of the cars above, the flecks of paint and rust and grease that automobiles shed just as animals shed hairs and breath and skin and dirt, and plants shed pollen and their own dead bodies, dried leaves and stems and stamens. The bagman swept it all into the brush without discrimination and pointed to the spot he'd cleared.

"You can rest here," he told the stranger. The stranger ignored him and lowered himself onto an unswept patch of ground. He leaned his back against a pillar, his package on his lap.

The bagman eyed the parcel, but kept sweeping until he had cleared another space a few feet away, this one somewhat larger to accommodate the bags. One by one, he carried them into this clearing. He laid them down with more ceremony than usual, making sure they stood straight, plumping each one like an overstuffed pillow. He stole a glance at the stranger, who was not looking at him at all, but was gazing upward at the glinting lens of the security camera mounted high in the groin of the overpass's concrete buttresses.

The bagman methodically emptied each bag, filling the space he'd swept with tidy piles. When he had removed everything, he began to rearrange his goods, shifting a sweater or a shredded spiral notebook or a plastic pirate's eye-patch from one stack to another, gazing each time at the brown parcel in the stranger's lap as if it were the pole star by which he oriented the entire operation, and at the stranger's eyes, to see if he was observing this display. He was not. This was hardly the tribunal the bagman had hoped for, but he continued nonetheless.

Some piles dwindled as others towered and finally tottered over and had to be built once more on firmer foundations. His classification schemes shifted by the minute. Sometimes he sorted by color or by size or material, plastics in one corner, paper goods in another, textiles in a third, but more often the criteria governing his decisions could not be immediately divined, and perhaps could not be communicated at all, or understood by anyone but him. After many rearrangings — his eyes all the while swiveling metronomically between the package on the stranger's lap and the stranger's absent gaze — he at last settled, brow knit with dissatisfaction, on an order that would temporarily suffice, that though it reached not even a base approximation of the desired ideal, would have to do for now. Forgoing any sign of approval or disapproval from his audience, the bagman carefully restuffed his bags according to this final esoteric taxonomy.

He left out only three objects: a blue plastic cigarette lighter, a package of frankfurters, and a green army blanket, more hole than wool, folded into a tight right triangle, like the flags that drape soldiers' caskets. The bagman tore through the plastic packaging with a fingernail and squeezed out a single wiggling frank, which he submitted for his guest's consideration with twofold intent: as an offering of food but also as a final display of evidence, as if to say, "Look. Look at this awful wagging thing. Look how wrong it is." The stranger acknowledged neither aspect of the bagman's oblation. He stared past the proffered frank, right through the bagman at the high grass swaying and crackling in the field behind him, so the bagman ate the thing himself.

The cough and the hum of rush-hour traffic began to fade, and with it the strength of the sun. A hummingbird darted from pillar to pillar, seeking nectar, but finding none. Its tiny green body shimmered pink, then blue, then a brilliant glowing gold before it hastened off into the weeds. In what remained of the light, the bagman gathered sticks and yellowed newspaper and the dry cardboard spine of a puddle-bloated roll of paper towels. He paced behind the stranger and gazed over his shoulder at the thing in his lap, its brown paper wrapping stained almost to translucence.

The bagman found a heavy log and dragged it through the bushes to their camp. He snapped it in two with a kick, arranged his kindling and with it lit a fire, fanning the smoke to keep it from the eyes of the stranger, who leaned against the pillar still, his jaw clenched, his knuckles white around his parcel. The bagman squeezed out another frank and roasted it over the fire, not even flinching when the flames licked at his fingertips, blackening his already blackened hands. The flesh of the frank charred and peeled and emitted little gusts of steam. The bagman offered it to the stranger, but the stranger again ignored him, so the bagman ate that one too.

When the sun had hidden itself entirely behind the pillars of the overpass where the freeway stretched off to the west, and the last of its light had fled from the gathering wind, the bagman unfolded his blanket and hung it over the stranger's shoulders. The stranger did not thank him, but spread the wormy thing over his lap to cover himself and the package that he held there. The bagman laid several sheets of newspaper on the ground, and laid himself atop them before they blew away. He shoved more newspapers into his sleeves and his pant legs, and laid out one final layer to pull over his shoulders before he curled himself into a ball on the ground, his face to the fire. He tried not to move at all, to mute the hysteric crinkling that accompanied his every tiny shift. He gazed off at the stranger behind the flames, still seated erect against his column, as if it were only through his efforts that it stayed standing and kept the freeway from tumbling to the earth. The bagman watched his new companion's eyes glow bright and orange in the firelight until at last he fell asleep.

Pigeon.

Pigeon woke before his sisters. The eldest lay curled beside him, humming in her sleep with her thumb in her mouth though she was three years older than Pigeon and Pigeon was almost nine already. Her shoulder blade jutted over her back like the joint of a folded wing. Pigeon had to unravel the littlest one's arm from his waist before he could rise to his knees and crawl out from beneath the sheet of tin under which they'd laid their mattress.

The dark had not yet lifted, but Pigeon had not slept well. For the first half of the night, he had been so excited about what he'd found that afternoon that he hadn't been able to sleep. The night seemed an unbearable imposition. Pigeon wondered if he should share his discovery with his sisters or keep it to himself. He worried that he might not be able to find it again. He knew that was absurd, that he could find it even in the moonless, un-starred night, but as he lay there on his skinny side between his sisters, to be extra sure that he did not forget, he traced the path again and again in his imagination, hoping to carve it into his brain, feeling right there on the mattress the sharp corners of the jumbled bricks through the thin soles of his shoes.

Sleep won out eventually. Pigeon dreamed of his mother. He was walking alone through a parking lot and saw his sisters in a car. They called to him. They were laughing. When he got close they rolled the window down and he saw that his mother was there behind the wheel. But when she saw him coming she pulled away. His sisters continued to laugh as she drove off. Pigeon woke in tears. He lay in the dark between his sisters, trying not to resent them for their behavior in his dream, trying also to remind himself of what the next day held. But the anguish of his dream stained everything. Insomniac Pigeon could imagine no acceptable escape, no possible distraction from this quivering abandonment, his solitary smallness on a planet much too large.

Sleep must have claimed him once again and spared him dreams, because the eastern sky was with apparent trepidation allowing itself to pinken at the rim, and Pigeon had no memory of the hours having passed. He rubbed his thin brown arms and stretched. The night was not cold, but his shirt was worn almost to translucence and standing now, without his sisters' bodies to warm him, he couldn't help but shiver. He caught his breath in his hands, hoping he would see it. But it was not cold enough for that. It was just breath. He walked out around behind the concrete slab and splashed urine on the dusty roots of an ole-ander. His pee didn't steam either. He tried to write his name, but he had started too late and he ran out before he finished dotting the *i*.

When Pigeon walked, and when he was nervous but standing still, his head bobbed back and forth, chin first. Pigeon was almost always nervous. Hence the name. But Pigeon's myriad fears had not stopped him before, and would not stop him now, in the thin, drooping light of the morning. He decided not to wake his sisters and not to share his discovery with them. Not today at least. He scampered off, chin abob, through the bushes and down along the trail to the edge of the lot.

Pigeon crawled through the brambles to the dirt road be-low and hurried along past the cedars and the strange pit behind them, past the chain-linked junkyard and under the bridge. His chin like a pendulum. He tried not to run and miss something important. You never knew where you'd find a portal, or what you'd have to do to open one. Kick a rock maybe, or circle three times, or maybe seven. It was best to try this with everything, to assume a certain esoteric structure to the cosmos, some hidden architectural order, and hence to always kick and circle and knock, to push anything that might be a button and pull any twig or protuberance that might be a lever in disguise, but right now Pigeon didn't have time.

Once he thought he had found one, when the three of them first explored the roofless concrete shed out where the chickens used to be. With fingers interwoven, his sister boosted Pigeon up to scramble over the edge of the cinderblock wall. The floor inside was strewn with mouse pellets, feathers, thousands of rusted nails, glass from the one high window. In a far corner he found a wide aluminum baking pan. Pigeon glanced inside it and saw a dark, concrete-walled passageway shimmering down beneath. His heart skipped. The other strata of the universe that Pigeon hoped to scale were always, in his imagination, better and more interesting than this one. If they proved frightening at times it was only to provide opportunities for heroism. Awash in awe, Pigeon leaned over the portal. A face blinked up at him. It was his own. He lowered a finger into the tin and saw a finger rise to meet him. His finger came back slick with a thick brown liquid. It was no passageway at all, just a tub of motor oil or some other viscous goo.

Pigeon cut through yards and shinnied over chain-link fences. He bobbed down an alley, counted his steps across an empty parking lot. And there it was, set in the middle of a yard heaped in wild disarray with broken red bricks, a strange gift for him and him alone. A trampoline. The frame and springs had only just begun to rust. The fabric was unfrayed. The sky was almost light now, the clouds pink and gold and gray. The sharp edges of the bricks dug through his thin-soled shoes. Pigeon hoisted himself aboard, tumbled towards the trampoline's center, pushed himself up on his elbows and stood. He jumped, let himself fall to his haunches, bounced to his feet. The frame creaked. He bounced higher and lifted his knees to his chest. With each jump, he bounced still higher. Pigeon stretched his skinny arms, reached for the low clouds above him, and jumped as high as gravity allowed.

He is consoled.

When the bagman awoke, tossed from his slumbers by the vibrations of a truck towing cattle on the overpass above, or by a rodent rustling in the bushes, or by the stranger's mumbled cries, it was the stranger he saw first, eyes closed tight, thin ribs aquiver beneath his tattered suit, fragmentary syllables tumbling from his lips. The fire had gone out. The bagman stood, his legs stiff from the cold and the hard ground and the paper stuffed inside his pants. He rearranged the blanket, which had fallen from the stranger's shoulders, peeking intently at the parcel beneath it as he did so. Crouching beside the stranger, he leaned his own broad back against the concrete pillar and wrapped a heavy arm around his comrade's shoulders.

"Don't you fret," the bagman whispered, and the stranger's proud head fell into the bagman's lap. A spasm shook the stranger's chest. Words the bagman could not comprehend spilled forth from sleep, the stranger's lips pulled white and thin over his perfect teeth. The bagman stroked the stranger's temples, smoothed his greasy hair against his soiled brow. "It don't matter," the bagman said. And while he comforted the stranger, he forgot for a while to covet the mysterious thing wrapped in brown paper that rested between the stranger's knees. With the backs of his filth-encrusted fingers, the bagman caressed the stranger's beard and hollow cheeks until the stranger's lips were still and his jaw unclenched and he slept peacefully there on the ground beneath the freeway, his head warm on the bagman's thigh.

Shortly before dawn, the stranger woke. The air was cold. His breath clouded out around him. Beside him lay the bagman.

He shoved the bagman's meaty arm from his chest and let it fall to the dirt. The bagman shifted and mumbled but did not awaken. The stranger rose, brushed the dust from his trousers and retrieved his package from the ground. He glanced down at the bagman wheezing in his grubby reindeer sweater, at the thread of drool hanging from his dark lips into the off-white thicket of his beard, at the three fat bags sitting dumb beside the ashes of the fire and at the flattened newspaper of the bagman's bed, now gray and wet with dew.

The stranger placed his package on the ground. He contemplated the camera mounted on the overpass above him, squinted at it, and proceeded to untie the string that bound the package he had retrieved from Gabriel's room. Without taking his eyes from the bagman's face, he reached beneath the brown paper wrapper. He cradled the parcel's content in his lap. He even stroked it some. The stranger looked at each of the bagman's eyes. The eyelids fluttered. He looked at the space between them, which was still. He considered the dark of the bagman's mouth, the rising mound of his gut, his beating heart. Through each and any of these spots on the bagman's body, death might easily be induced to enter. As if being so beheld disturbed his sleep, the bagman stirred. He coughed again. He pawed at his groin and farted sweetly.

The stranger pursed his lips, then smiled. "Not you," he whispered. "Not now." He replaced the package's contents, tied the string over the paper once more, kicked a rock into the bushes, and walked away.

TWO

I dream dreams.

Eventually I sleep. Exhaustion wins. I dream dreams of insects burrowing, of false teeth, of rootless trees falling sequentially, each in a different direction, their trunks like fingers pointing, accusing. I don't dream of him at all. Though it's dark still, at least one bird is up. I think it's a magpie from the sounds it makes. It has chosen a branch on the laurel tree just outside our bedroom window. It sits there and complains. Even birds have complaints. There's never enough bugs to go round. The sky is too low. Eggs aren't what they once were. The oppressive conformity of flocking. Every four seconds — I count — the bird sounds the same shrill, harrying call. I wouldn't call it a song. Like this: One, two, three, four, to weet, to weet, to woo. One, two, three, four, to weet, to weet, to woo.

I try for a while to slip back to sleep, but the bird is too damn loud and too persistent. It has to have its say. I give up. I crane my neck and lift the blinds, but I can't see it out the window. What would I do, anyway, if I could see it? Throw a rock at it? I don't have a rock, and there's the screen in the way, and even if I could kill the thing I still wouldn't be able to get back to sleep. Beside me, she stirs but doesn't wake. I stand and watch her for a moment, her face alone exposed above the sheets. She frowns and chews at something in her sleep. She rubs her nose. I close the bedroom door behind me.

Then I do what I do in the morning. I brush my teeth. I consider flossing and decide I'd rather not. I run the shower and scrub the night from my body. I soap my face, my chest, my feet. The places where night collects. Between the toes — it'll stay there all day long if you're not careful. I dry myself, rub on lotion so that my skin won't furrow and decay any faster than it has to, deodorant so that I won't prematurely stink. I coax the wax from my ears with a Q-tip. I comb my hair. I see the stranger in the mirror, standing behind me while I shave. His hands are at his sides. I nod and keep on shaving. He doesn't nod back. When I turn of course he's gone.

I dress and leave the house, lock the door and take the bus. The sun is rising. I stare out the graffiti-scratched windows, at the chewing gum dried to the bolts on the floor. The sunlight filters in like mist. In the seat behind me, a white-bearded man snores. No, it's not him, and not the other one. This one has no teeth, carries no bags, and wears no tattered suit, just turquoise sweatpants and a bright pink t-shirt that reads, "It's not a bald spot — it's a solar panel for a sex machine." Though he is not even a little bit bald.

The elevator's broken again, so I climb the stairs again. Seven flights. I'm panting when I dig the key from my pocket to unlock my office door. The floor is littered with junk mail the postman shoved beneath the door. Credit card offers, office-supply catalogs, takeout menus. Deadly stuff. I leave it all there. The sun slants in thick and yellow through the blinds. Weird ochre trapezoids drift across the wall. This is where I sit and write to you, where I typed the page you're reading now. I switch on the computer. It stares at me. I stare back. "We could do this all day," I tell it.

Outside, I can hear a preacher warming up. Most mornings, there's a preacher in the park. This one expounds in blunt, staccato Spanish, his voice distorted by the squawk of the megaphone and the shifting wind and the brick walls of the buildings that stand between my window and the park. "Why do you walk the paths of sin?" he asks, but he's not asking really. He's not waiting for an answer. "Where will you store the wages of your unrighteousness?" Don't count on my translations. I'm mainly guessing here. But I know I have the next line right. "Dios es amor," he shouts, "y todo el amor que nosotros tenemos pertenece a dios, todo el amor que nosotros sentimos viene de dios, porque dios es amor y nos quiere el señor."

The funny thing is that the tone and the pitch of his voice do not shift at all when he gets to the bit about god being love. It's all of a piece. That same squealing scold. Elementary kerygmatics, to weet, to weet, to woo. God is love, man undeserving. Stones are rock and rocks are stones. Fish and clods of earth are innocent. So are molecules of air. Man is perfect and pure. Man is love perhaps and god is vicious and corrupt. Animals are dumber than they look. Illness is spread via miasma, proximity to corpses, the evil eye. The distance between man and god is measured in sin. But whose sin, god's or man's? Volume is measured in pecks and pints and sometimes jeroboams. Depth in fathoms, life in fingernails and orgasms and other people's funerals. Water is fluid except when it's ice. Days end in evenings. Stars are always, always far away. Form is emptiness and emptiness form. Time a species of madness. Faith too. And lack of faith.

I keep a couch in my office, a little bookcase, some instant coffee and a hot plate. The stranger's lying on the couch. He wasn't there a second ago, but he is now, with his feet up on the corner of my desk. He's leafing through my dictionary.

"Your feet," I say.

He looks up as if surprised to see me. "Do you know what fulminic means?" he asks after a moment.

"No," I say. He moves his feet.

I brush flakes of mud from the corner of my desk. Outside, the preacher says something about sin, and something more about it. Pecado pecado vicio pecado. It's hard to make out the rest. His bullhorn squeals. Its volume wavers. "Él regresará," he says. He will return and walk among us. Then the megaphone goes silent. Snack time for the prophet. So much good news takes its toll.

"What do you think?" I ask the stranger.

"What do I think about what?"

"About what he says." I hook a thumb at the window to indicate the park below.

The stranger closes the dictionary, places it like a pillow beneath his head. He lifts one nostril, shrugs. "Not much."

"That's all," I say. "Not much?"

"What about 'fugacious'?" he says.

I swivel in my chair to face him. "Fleeting," I say, "like sunsets, and lightning, and love. Like patience. Did you come here for a reason?"

"Don't be coy," he replies. "I could ask you the same question."

"You could," I admit. "Do you have anything to say?"

"I'm saying it," he answers.

62

"You're not saying anything."

He raises an eyebrow, grunts, bored. I toss a paper clip at him. It hits him in the nose. He doesn't blink. I ask him if he wants to wrestle. He doesn't hear me, or pretends he doesn't. I repeat myself. "Do you want to wrestle?"

He picks the paper clip up off his knee, where it has fallen, twists it straight, and returns it to my desk. He makes a face. "Wrestle you?"

"Yeah. Me."

He shakes his head, annoyed. "No," he says.

"What then?"

But he doesn't answer, and when I look again he's gone. The dictionary is still there on the couch, open to the Fs.

I see the preacher later when I head downstairs for breakfast. I'm pretty sure it's him. From the sidewalk, I spot him through the pharmacy's automatic doors. A short man, with a peasant's lanky walk. His hair combed flat against his head. He wears a brown suit that doesn't fit him. Cuffs down almost to his thumbs. A megaphone hangs by the strap from one wrist. He's laughing and flirting with the cashier. He mops at his forehead with a blue bandanna and buys a pack of batteries. She pushes his change across the counter, smiles shyly. Brakes screech behind me. A car hits a pigeon with a greasy thud. It lands in a shower of its own feathers on the sidewalk and lies there, eyes open, as if it's got something hard to think about. Something that can't wait. The preacher steps out of the store, grinning. The stranger, behind him, winks.

The light.

She had strayed too far. The dawn had come on with sudden violence, as if the horizon had been lit aflame. The warehouses were beginning to awaken. Just now, a truck had almost hit her. She couldn't hear it of course, for she could not hear anything, but she felt the weight of it shake the asphalt and she felt the heat of it and when she turned it was just feet behind her, the red-faced driver shouting something from the cab. She pulled her shirts about her and hurried towards home.

The hummingbird had died. She had tied a stocking around it so that its broken wing would not dangle. She had tried to feed it. She cut a ripe pear into hummingbird-size bits, but it would not take them. She walked a mile to the all-night liquor store and did not have to pretend not to hear the clerk yelling at her as she filled her pockets with packets of sugar. Pack by pack, she stirred the sugar into a mug filled with water from the drainpipe. She let the solution drip from her finger into the hummingbird's beak. It would not swallow. She even gathered flowers — first more cast-off bouquets from outside the warehouse and later, when the bird ignored those, on the theory that wildness was a requirement of its nutrition, she plucked bougainvillea blossoms and the morning glories that climbed the chain-link fence above the embankment, poppies from the secret patch behind the high grass in the field beside the chroming shop, jasmine from the hedge in someone's yard. She tied the stocking to a post outside so the bird could hang and almost fly. She waved the flowers one by one beneath it. But the bird disdained to acknowledge her offerings.

On the morning of the third day, its little bowstring of a heart ceased quivering.

She couldn't bear the thought of burying it, of sticky dirt on its bright plumage, eternal interment for a thing meant to fly. Rodents might find it. Worms would be sure to. Death and stillness had rendered the bird heavy. She wanted to make it light again. She soaked the stocking in rubbing alcohol and tried to burn the hummingbird over a matchbox pyre. The flames danced, then guttered out before the feathers were even singed. She poured on more alcohol, with the same result.

With the bird once again lodged in her pocket, she walked out to the gas station, farther than the liquor store. She retrieved a plastic pop bottle from the trash and waited for a customer. The first four who came refused her entreaties or pretended not to understand them, silent, gestural and panicked as her attempts at communication were. The fifth arrival smiled at her from the seat of his idling Toyota. He wore a trim goatee and a security guard's uniform and his eyes were rimmed with red. "How you doing, Lilith?" he said, nodding as if he knew her. "What's going on, baby?" Of course she could not hear him.

The goateed man pulled a half-liter Evian bottle from the cup-holder beside him and took a long swallow of a foamy pinkish liquid. He squinted his eyes, jerking his head spasmodically about. He let out a long, slow whistling breath and offered the bottle to the woman through his window. She shook her head. He opened the door and lifted himself from his seat, groaning. His shirt was untucked. He put a hand out, beckoning with one crooked finger. "C'mere now, Lilith," he said. "Just a lil' bit closer."

The woman didn't move.

The goateed man's eyes glowed with a watery sort of light. He tugged one ear and then the other. A smile tore suddenly at his face. Like a gymnast preparing for a leap, he pumped his arms twice at his sides and leaned back so far that the woman feared he would hit his head on the door of the car behind him. Then, like a rubber band stretched to its limit and released, he whipped forward again, bending at the waist and jumping now, hopping up and down on the heels of both black-sneakered feet, grabbing at the air and on the backswing squeezing his hands into fists. "Shock 'n' awe, baby!" he yelled. "C'mere, Lilith! Let's make a fucking party! I'm gonna call you Shock 'n' Motherfuckin' Awe!"

She did not wait for him to step toward her. She aimed one sharp kick between his legs. The impact hurt her toes, but she ran anyway, clutching her skirts and the tiny dead bird in her pocket until she was beyond the reach of the fluorescent light that illuminated the pumps. She hid crouched in the bushes, trying not to move, waiting for her heart to slow, watching the goateed man leap about, red-faced now and sweating, howling and spitting and shadow boxing, drop kicking the air, head-butting it, hooting triumphantly and stomping his feet. Eventually the man grew winded. He pumped his gas and drove away.

She waited until three more cars had come and gone before she emerged again from the brush. Only later, after four additional strangers had rejected her mute requests, did she encounter a willing accomplice, a little boy. He was topping off the tank of his father's truck while the father used the restroom. Perhaps unaware of gasoline's forbidden stupefactory potential and heedless of his parents' oft-repeated injunctions regarding strangers, the boy allowed the woman to approach and fill her bottle from the pump.

The hummingbird burned with an eager blue flame. She crouched and watched the smoke pour from its tiny form. When it had been entirely consumed and the flames, lacking further fuel, died down, she blew the ashes into the breeze and crawled into her bed. For nearly a week, she did not get out again except to squat in the dirt outside. She dreaded even that brief contact with the open air.

But she realized eventually that if she did not force herself to get up, she simply never would, that only motion could pull her out of this. It did, and here she was as a result of its predation, caught by the approach of daylight, rushing homeward. The streets were already crowded with wheeling forklifts, men pushing handcarts, trucks in slow reverse. The buildings yawned, their mouths uncovered. The shutters above the loading bays had been rolled away and here and there between the trucks she caught a peek inside the warehouses: high-ceilinged expanses stacked to the roof beams with row upon row of crated goods, lit in a pale fluorescent windowless green. She dodged her way through the throng. Everyone ignored her. A pickup truck squeezed through the alley and nudged her aside with its bumper. Her hands began to tremble. A man, arms filled with boxes, backed into her and knocked her down without pausing to see what or whom he'd hit.

Kneeling where she'd fallen, on one knee and with her palm against the street, she found that she was crying. She'd scraped the knee and maybe bruised an elbow — but it wasn't that. The shock of the fall dislodged something in her, shook loose a stopper somewhere, and the tears rolled from her eyes.

She stood. The sky was nearly light now. A semi steamed past just inches from her shoulder. A small gaggle of men laughing and drinking coffee from paper cups approached, briefly engulfed her, and walked on. The world moved through her like a river through a net. Her chin was wet. She swabbed at her cheeks with the heel of her hand.

The woman did not feel sorry for herself. She could not complain of her deaf ears or her mute tongue, of her poverty or her solitude. These things had long been hers. Nor did she mourn the hummingbird. It was only a bird. Birds die. What she felt was something more diffuse, an ache carved out by all the rush and tumble of the universe, all its carelessness and the loneliness of things — not just the living and the sentient but the entire silent world of objects — cinder blocks, books, exhaust pipes. She could find no solidarity there. Everything was alone, everything misplaced. Everything was lost. The bird was not special. Nor was she.

She pushed her way out of the alleys and made a dash across the lots. The landscape now seemed soaked in sadness, saturated, as if sorrow were the one thing that held it all together, that saved the world from dissolution, preventing all its constituent particles from spinning off to stake their claims alone. Telephone wires hung from the poles along the avenues and even the arc of them, the receding, conjoining lines of them, seemed to tell a story of aloneness and loss.

She reached the fence. She was almost home. She looked back. The sun had risen from behind a cloud and was high enough now to light those wires so that they looked like filaments of gold leading off to some less doleful place. The dust raised by the passing trucks glowed gold as well. The cars in the lots glittered. Their hubcaps shone. The rooflines of the warehouses too, and every east-facing wall was remade by the dawn, gilded and bright, as if everything had been lit quietly aflame. Then the woman did a funny thing. She laughed. She wiped her nose and laughed. For all the light's auroral trickery, the world seemed no less drenched with grief. But it was also something else, something almost complete and almost beautiful, but just beyond her reach.

He goes a'rambling.

The sun rose higher and the stranger's suit, heavy and wet with dew, soon dried. His limbs loosened with the warmth. Insects woke by the millions and commenced to rub together their wings and their hairy stick-like legs, celebrating the heat of another day with a vast and undulating buzz as the stranger strolled back toward the city. He crossed the field of brambles through which the bagman had led him and there collected on his pants and on his socks and in the callused flesh of his ankles dozens of barbed golden spurs. He picked them off and found the old empty dog track, its high walls adorned with blackened glass tubes once alive with neon light, dim now but still twisted in the shape of racing greyhounds. He pushed through the rusted gate. The track had grown over with thistle and dandelion. Half the terraced wooden seats were splintered, smashed. Vines snaked across the scoreboard. In a corner on the ground over where the concession stand had been, among shards of glass in a dozen shades of brown and green, the stranger found the remains of the mechanized rabbit, once the root of so much fuss, torn now from its track, fur worn away and matted, one ear gone. He nudged it with his toe. What fur remained fell off, revealing wood and wire. He kicked at the rabbit's wire-stuffed head and watched it bounce across the dirt.

The stranger walked on until he found the train yards. He sat on a railroad tie and tossed a rock from palm to palm until among all the sleepy freights a commuter train zipped past, the sunlight bouncing off its tinted windows, blinding him. He stood and followed the tracks on which it ran out away from the city. The stranger kicked a stone in front of him, whistled a tune low into his beard. The tracks ran through block-long plains of rubble where brown brick apartment buildings had once towered. They skirted the base of a pyramidal mountain of trash fringed with soft green grass. Gulls screamed in the air above. One clutched a chicken bone in its beak. The others harried and attacked it. The stranger did not look up. The tracks took him past yawning sand pits, truck yards behind barbed wire, the back doors of machine shops, rendering plants, shooting ranges, a brothel decked out in blue and violet neon. He came upon a boy leaping high on a trampoline set alone in the center of a field of broken bricks. He paused. The boy had not seen him. The stranger shifted his parcel from arm to arm. He tugged lightly at the string that bound it. The boy pulled his knees to his chest as he rose. His eyes rolled upwards, rapt. The stranger considered him for a moment, then retied the parcel and walked straight on.

At last he reached a trestle where the tracks passed over a wide suburban street, empty, at this hour, of cars. He scrambled down the embankment to the road and caught his pant leg on a root, tore off half a cuff, cursed. A mile down that road he turned onto a smaller road, and from there onto a smaller road still, not paved but dirt and rutted. There he found a small clapboard house, paint peeling, windows boarded up. A camera was still mounted on the eaves above the door, but it did not blink or hum and its lens was furred with grime. The stranger sat on a log in the shade behind the house, facing a wide and overgrown lawn. Roses, untended, bloomed on woody, head-high stalks. Tomato vines had leapt from their cages and covered half the yard. The fruits hung red and heavy, dripping, entrails exposed by birds. He untied his shoes. They were ankle-high calfskin lace-ups with dainty inch-high heels and soles now paper-thin. He shook a rock or two from each one, poured the sand from his socks, and picked what dirt and lint he could dislocate from the spans between his toes. A grasshopper settled on his knee, a shocking green, but it leapt away before his hand could reach it.

When he had rested for a while, the stranger retied the laces of his shoes and untied the twine that bound his treasured package. He unfolded the brown paper wrapping, exposing his possession to the sun, the clouds, the high branches of the trees. He searched around for prying eyes and cameras, but found none, and lifted the thing in both his hands. I'll tell you what it is and was, but that alone won't tell you much. It was a weapon, but not like any other. In the overhanging shadow of the eaves, it looked almost dull, no color at all, no shine to it, not like the sexy things that sulk blued beneath the gunshop glass, but like something baked from clay or ash, or carved from lifeless flesh, which after all is kin to ash and clay.

The thing had a barrel short and snubbed, but with a twist and a shake of the wrist it telescoped out to cartoon proportions, longer than the stranger's forearm and wider than his wrist. Its magazine swelled like a grooved balloon. It looked to have had a stock once, but it was broken off and jagged still at the break. The grip had been repaired with masking tape, now worn almost black with grit and sweat and ancient blood except here and there where it was newly patched with red electric tape.

In the light though, when the stranger stepped a few feet forward, the thing looked like it was made of glass, or of some crystal of impossible quality, reflecting every color in the spectrum and a few you haven't thought of, and when the stranger flicked his wrist again it looked more sword than gun, long as a broomstick and edged so sharp it would slice your eyes to see it. And when he pointed it at a squirrel in a faraway tree, it was suddenly a fearsome ax, blade curled like the crescent moon and near as big, dripping light and weight and death. When he twirled it like a cheerleader's baton between his fingers that blade condensed to a spearhead, black and slender but still boastful of its cruelty. And when he shifted it from hand to hand it shrank in size to almost nothing, something for a lady's handbag, a little scratchy peashooter, good for fending off drunks and the smaller variety of muggers. He spun and tossed it like a TV Wyatt Earp, but what he caught was just a penknife with broken blade and rusted hinge, capable of spreading tetanus if no quicker death. The stranger closed his fist, and if you had the strength and opportunity to pry it open, you'd find inside those long fingers nothing more than a plain old stone, a flat dull pebble, a shard of bone, some earth.

73

Relief.

The bagman woke and found himself alone. He rose hurriedly and searched the perimeter of his camp, pushing clumps of reeds aside to look between them, sliding his bags across the concrete to inspect the ground beneath. He found nothing. The stranger had left nothing behind, and yet everything seemed changed. If the material world had before felt imperfectly formed to the point of actual satire, now, in the wake of this encounter, it felt shabbier than ever, cheapened. The bagman recalled the stillness with which the stranger had sat on the swaying bus, as if he were invisibly rooted to some anchor deep below the earth, or conversely, as if he were himself the weight of a pendulum suspended from the clouds, impervious to mere terrestrial inertia. And he recalled the thing the stranger had carried as if it had been some golden scepter or an emerald larger than his head and not a plain parcel wrapped in stained brown paper and tied with kitchen twine. It was perfect, the bagman thought, a perfect thing.

The bagman skipped his usual morning ablutions and immediately set about sweeping clear a larger square of concrete. He folded the newspapers on which he'd slept, tossed them in the bushes, and removed his possessions piece by piece from the plastic bags that held them. He laid them side by side in a wide circle around the camp and spiraled them in toward the firepit. Among quite a few additional objects, he produced a fan belt; a pair of sunglasses; a ballpoint pen; a pencil sharpener; a volleyball; a balaclava; two bungee cords, red and white; a coconut; a plastic fork; a skull-shaped stone; three varieties of seashells; an unrolled condom, dried to the consistency of beachstrewn kelp; a fez; a pair of mittens; a yellow legal pad; a purple bandanna; a maple leaf; a plastic owl; a postcard depicting three baboons; an aluminum hose-clamp; a box of sugared cereal; a small plush monkey, missing one ear; a rusted can opener; a plastic action figure gripping a scimitar with tiny yellow hands; the cast-off exoskeleton of a locust; the Book of Mormon; a magic eight-ball; a creased watercolor of a sunset; a paisley necktie; the dry stone of an apricot; a pornographic magazine, the cover of which bore the words "The Beaver Twins: Wide Open"; a lumpy pearl; three pebbles of unusual color and shape; a toothbrush still wrapped in its cellophane packaging; a pair of crew socks; a coffee mug that announced itself to be the World's #1 Granny; a Y-shaped twig; the dried foot of a seagull; an empty green bottle that had once contained aftershave lotion; a spark plug; a magnifying glass; an unopened box of bandaids, a glass shaker filled with crushed red pepper; a dog whistle that had never been used to call a dog; a pair of handcuffs, *sans* key; the crushed ribs and vertebrae of a garter snake preserved in a ziplock bag; a hearing aid; a hand towel; a small, faded plastic pumpkin; two unmatching sandals; a sweatshirt advertising a company that manufactures sweatshirts; two wedding rings, one bent; and a single bobby pin.

When he had emptied all three bags, the bagman's possessions lay helixed about beneath the overpass like a crop circle, but even this impressive arrangement gave him no pleasure. All spread out like that, the pale tawdriness of his things — and of all things, not just the pumpkin, the monkey and the twig, but the concrete they lay on, the cracks in it, the pillars that supported the highway above him, the highway itself, the reeds and trash-strewn bushes — seemed only to have multiplied. He considered rearranging it all in a pyramid, or something close to a cube, but dismissed both ideas as futile. Nothing could redeem these things. There was no magic order, no code to break or secret lock to pick. All context was equally empty, for all its possible components were empty too. They were already their own ghosts, these things, their own crinkled husks. But the bagman knew one thing that wasn't.

He turned and walked away. He could not remember the last time he had taken three steps without his bags. He felt almost weightless. He wanted to skip. His eyes seemed to allow more light into his brain. He remembered the name of this sensation. It was not quite freedom: it was called relief. He kicked a rock from his path and broke into a bent, lumbering sprint.

He made it halfway across the field. The light had grown too bright inside his skull. His heart thumped. His mouth was dry. He couldn't breathe. He was a large man, and far from young, so maybe it was the effort of running fast. But maybe it was something else. Maybe he could no longer allow himself to live unburdened. A wave of nausea overtook him, and he remembered. He had made a deal. What was his was no longer his. It wasn't even his to leave behind.

The bagman recovered his breath and walked back with eyes downcast. He retrieved the things from the ground and stuffed them into the bags, but not with any care and not in any special order. He just stuffed them in.

He is challenged.

The stranger sat there kneeling, the stained brown paper empty at his ankle beside him. Between his palms he held the thing. His mouth hung agape and his eyes shone with something very much like love. He stroked it as you might caress an infant, caressing not just the humble thing itself but the luminous and empyrean future that it promised to call forth, and the past it could not fail to redeem. He was lost in it. The voices, when at last he heard them, arrived as if from somewhere far away.

"You old bum!" said one voice.

"Faggot!" said another.

"Stinking perv!" a third voice said.

"Dirty old bum!" the first chimed in again.

Across the yard the stranger spied a clump of boys in windbreakers and baseball caps worn backwards. He grinned and counted them. One. Two. Three. The fourth a fat one. The stranger rose, his eyes dancing with delight. Four boys. Foul-mouthed boys, ill-bred and nasty-minded. Nothing more corrupt than children. As good a place to start as any. He lifted the thing in his fist and with a steady hand took aim first at the one farthest from him, a fat boy hanging back a bit, fumbling in the pockets of his baggy shorts. But before the stranger could execute his wishes, something hit him in the ribs. As he stepped back a second stone struck him hard in the wrist. He tripped over the log behind him and, falling, lost his grip on the thing in his hand. It fell in the grass out of his sight. He hissed a curse.

"You got him!" said the first voice.

"I got him too!" said another.

"Hit him again!" the third boy said.

"Don't be a faggot, Tubs. Throw the fucking rock!" yelled the first boy to the fourth.

The boys let loose another volley of stones and it was the fat one this time who hit his mark, striking the stranger on the temple with a chunk of granite as big as a fist.

"Hah!" the fat boy yelled, pumping his chubby fist, "Who's the faggot now?"

The stranger groaned and groped in the weeds. At last his fingers found what they were searching for, but by the time he stood and blinked away the blood in his eyes enough to be able to aim, the boys had scattered through the trees.

"Bum!" yelled one boy, his voice trailing off as he dived over a hedge.

"Old bum!" yelled another, diving after him.

"Who's the faggot now?" howled the fat boy with glee as he followed his friends to safety.

Mice.

The slenderest of the three sat shirtless over his needlepoint. He was quite tall, and heavily tattooed with lightning bolts and crosses. A panther crawled up his arm. An eagle spread its wings across his shoulders. A cartoon woodpecker winked just below his navel. He sat on a trunk, his pale collarbones jutting, red suspenders hanging at his sides. As he stitched, a flush of pride spread across his cheeks and upwards, even to the peak of his shining, hairless skull. "Almost done," he announced in a whisper that barely contained his excitement.

In front of him, a short and rotund but solid man, similarly inked but with his red suspenders pulled up over a sleeveless undershirt, shaved the cratered, pink scalp of a third man, tall, thick-necked, and fat. The taller man sat on a metal folding chair, which, beneath him, looked to have been burgled from a doll's house. He was dressed like his companions in black jeans and high, shiny, red-laced boots.

"Where do you get that?" the seated man said, suddenly annoyed by the tall and skinny man's pronouncement. "It's not one yet. It's not even nine."

"Stay still," scolded the short and fat man. He stood back to examine his work and hone his razor across a leather strop. "If you keep moving I'll chop your scars off."

"Go on," said the tall and fat.

"Your scalp," went on the short and fat, "has more potholes, pimples and pockmarks than your mother's carbuncled ass. Did you know that?"

His comrade responded obliquely: "Did you know that a

moray eel's teeth are so filled with rotting bits of fish-flesh that if one bites you, you're sure to get septicemia and die within moments of an agonizing death? Did you know that? Did you know you look like one, that if you only had a neck you'd look exactly like a green moray eel?"

The tall and skinny guffawed. "Tell him about the sea snakes."

"They don't live in lakes, idiot," replied the tall and fat. "They live under rocks in the ocean. Twelve feet long. Covered in slime. The green morays have blue skin, but they appear to be green due to the slime that coats them. Lots of funny fishes in the sea. Sea snakes, for instance. Most common marine reptile there is. Closely related to their terrestrial cousins. Can be nine feet long. They hunt underwater, surface for air. Sailors sometimes see big balls of them, hundreds of them smarming about in one humongous ball. Ouch." He slapped at the short man's calf and rubbed at his head, checking his fingers for blood. "Watch that. I have a blemish up there."

"A what?" the shorter man inquired. "I hope you didn't say you have a blemish. Your whole head is a blemish. A blemish balanced on top of a blemish that blemishes about on two long, bloated blemishes."

The tall and thin looked up from his stitching. "Flemish," he said, and giggled to himself.

The tall and fat continued. "They travel in hordes, sea snakes. Big messes of them, bands one hundred feet wide and seven miles long across the water, nothing but snakes by the millions slithering through the waves. And their poison, get this, is eight times more poisonous than the venom of a king cobra. Ten times more than a rattler's. One drop is enough to kill three men and most times they bite they inject five drops at least. So you're done for if one gets you. Sea snakes. God's creatures. Wonders of the deep."

He ran a palm over his scalp, scouting for nicks and missed patches of hair. The shorter man smacked it away.

"Then there's the blue-ringed octopus," the tall and fat went on. "No bigger than a golf ball but it carries enough venom to kill twenty-six men. Maculotoxin, it's called. Like tetrodotoxin, that the puffer fish have. Ten thousand times more deadly than cyanide. Blocks the neural pathways. You don't stand a chance. Pretty little things though. They glow blue when they're excited. You can't imagine a more attractive cephalopod."

The thin man pulled his needle down through the canvas and tied off the final strand of his design. "There," he said, and turned it around for his companions to see. "What do you think?"

On a white background, surrounded by a crude border of death's heads, pink carnations, and paired red lightning bolts, he had stitched two words in sharp Teutonic script.

The short and fat paused his barbering and scratched at the hinge of his jaw. "Judo Maus," he said. "What's that?"

"It means, 'white pride,' I think. Or 'white power,'" the tall and skinny beamed. "Or 'fuck all Jews,' something like that. It's German."

"Who told you that?"

"Not Gujarat. Fuck no. In German. That one we met at the club last week who just came back from Leipzig, he kept saying it: *judo maus*. White power!" He shouted and punched at the ceiling for emphasis. "Where should we put it up?"

The tall and fat stood suddenly. All three men kicked their

heels in unison, and threw their right hands in the air. The short and fat clenched his straight razor in his fist. Together they saluted, "Judo maus!"

The folding chair creaked as the tall and fat took his seat once more. He indicated the far wall of the room with a nod. "Hang it above the chaise lounge," he said. "With the others."

He is filled with wrath.

He could no longer see the boys. Even their shouts and gig-gles had faded, so the stranger aimed at the unkempt hedge over which the four had leaped. It shivered, and for a second it seemed to even bleed. It glowed orange for a moment, every last twig of it, then fell away, just ash. He took aim at a tree beside the hedge. Its leaves slipped from its branches and the bare trunk danced like a hair held over a flame, then disap-peared. The stranger reduced every tree in sight to black and sticky dust. A cypress, two oaks, some pepper trees. He burned the grass and the weeds and the abandoned house behind him. With a screech that sounded as if it came from a living thing, the windows shivered, then burst. He burned the rocks and the fallen branches and fallen leaves and the snails and beetles and spiders and worms that made their homes there. He scorched the earth itself, every ditch and lump and pebble, until it bled and pussed and healed hard and sharp as glass, so that no living thing would ever wish to walk on it, and no seed would ever think to germinate there.

When he was done, he gazed around him at the smoking ruins. A breeze still blew. From somewhere he could hear a si-ren. He didn't feel any better, so he kicked a hot and blackened rock, and broke his toe, then yelled and limped away before the fire department came.

I feel a little sick.

I'm halfway home when the stranger stops me on the sidewalk. It hasn't been the best of mornings. I paid the rent and I'm pretty sure the check won't bounce, but I forgot to pack a lunch so I'm walking home to save the five dollars a sandwich would cost me, plus another three bucks for round-trip bus fare. I'm almost dizzy from adding and subtracting numbers in my head, checking and rechecking columns, trying to figure out what it'll take to get through the month, so I'm happy, in a way, for the distraction, if hardly in the mood to justify myself. But this is none of your business. Really. He stands in front of me, his arms akimbo. He's whistling softly to himself and tapping his right foot.

I step around him. The stranger turns and walks beside me. He rests his left hand on my right shoulder. It is not an affectionate gesture. "Tell me something," he says, and squeezes hard.

I twist away to shake his hand off. "No hello?" I say. "No how are you?"

"Hello how are you," he says. He smiles flatly, a little too quickly to come off as nonchalant.

"Shitty," I answer. "But thanks for asking. What do you want to know?"

"Where is this going?" he asks.

"This?" I say.

He waves his hand at the sidewalk to indicate the path before him. "This," he says.

"Don't you know?"

"How could I?"

"Because you're the one who's going there."

"You're not funny," the stranger says.

I shrug. I didn't mean to be funny. We reach the corner. The light is red. A few yards to our right, a dog in the yard of a transmission shop barks behind a chain-link fence. It's a chow, its greasy fur matted in uneven auburn dreadlocks, black gums drawn back and howling. Clearly, it would kill us if it could. The notion of a world beyond the fence, of creatures free to move about the world at will, is apparently too much for it.

The stranger ignores the dog. "You're not going to answer me?" he asks.

"Should I?"

"You should."

"Why?"

"Because I asked." He seems quite sure of this.

I smile. "Not good enough," I say. The stranger stares at me, his eyes aflame. I want to laugh, but don't. Really, I don't want to be cruel. Or not gratuitously so. The chow keeps snapping at the chainlink. It's foaming at the mouth. I don't feel good about this. In fact I feel a little sick.

"Are we wrestling now?" he asks.

"Yes," I try to smile. "We're wrestling." The light changes. The sign says WALK. I walk. He's not beside me anymore. I don't look back.

I take the side streets. I return to my worries. They waited for me. I do the math. I leap a puddle at the entrance to an alley and watch two sparrows fight inside an empty bag of cheese puffs. The bag twists and crinkles and jerks as if driven by some invisible conglomeration of gears, or by its own bumbling baggish will. One of the birds expels the other. It emerges dredged in day-glo orange dust, and flies away. For a second, I'm jealous of its flight. Maybe for longer than a second. Then the other sparrow flies away. The wind takes over where the birds left off, lifting the bag in the air.

I turn a corner and another corner and climb the last block up the hill to my house. Her car is not in the driveway. The house will be empty. I'm hungry, and can't remember what's in the fridge. Peanut butter if nothing else. I lift the latch to the low wrought-iron gate and close it again behind me. Of course the stranger's there already, pacing on my porch, his arms behind his back. He's not whistling anymore.

"I won't ask twice," he says.

"That's fine," I tell him, digging into my pocket for the key.

A dog trots past on the sidewalk behind me, its nose to the concrete. Its coat is speckled, almost blue. Tail busy, ears alert. If dogs can smile, it's smiling. A loose-lipped piebald grin. It lifts a leg and dribbles piss on the gardenias. The stranger croaks out something like a laugh. "This time," he says, "you're the one behind the fence."

"Look around," I say. "Where are you?"

Rush hour.

The bagman stood on the corner. It was the time of morning known colloquially as rush hour, when the world fades to blur and humankind is granted collective license not to notice its surroundings, to gaze upon creation with the utmost pragmatism, regarding all objects solely as potential obstacles. This is a bad time. Motion is all that matters at this hour, and motion is what occurs, a mass, one-way migration. The endpoint of this pilgrimage, be it office, kitchen or factory floor, is the single image permitted to float before the mind's eye, odious though that image may be to its bearer. So the bagman, though he formed an island — an archipelago, if you count his three lumped bags — in a veritable sea of pedestrians, was for all intents and purposes, despite his girth, his appearance and his unorthodox scent, invisible.

He stood and watched the throng surge past. Men in suits bustled officiously by, and men in pressed khakis, and in canvas coveralls. Women in heels and binding skirts of worsted wool clicked past, and some in blue jeans, and in the pink and white uniforms of maids. None slumped. All held their shoulders high and chins forward as if hooked by the collar and pulled workward by a covert network of the slenderest monofilament. The bagman, who had once upon a long-lost time been one of them, watched in awe. How religiously they must regard creation to be able to march so surely through it, and to ignore it so completely.

The bagman slumped. He scratched himself. He belched and belched again, loudly. No one looked his way. On the opposite corner, across a clogged river of howling, honking cars, one figure stood out. One man stood still, a tall and almost skeletally thin man wearing thick eyeglasses over clear, blue eyes of an almost shocking innocence. He had a long, pale face that looked like it had been carved with dull tools from a tree trunk. His hair was red and curly and unevenly styled, as if he had attempted to paste it flat against his skull with gel, but had lost interest halfway through. Around his neck hung a choker of black-rimmed camera lenses strung with kitchen twine. Beneath that a loosely knotted tie. He wore a sandwich-board over his clothes and held a megaphone before his lips. He appeared to be preaching. Don't confuse him with the man I heard preaching through my window. This was a different sort of preacher. He did not mention love at all. Or even sin.

From across the avenue, the bagman could not hear a word he said, and could not make out the text printed on his board. The sun glinted off the lenses around the preacher's neck, blinding the bagman. Intrigued, he shouldered his bags and when the light changed, he joined the rushing masses and crossed the street.

The bagman sat on the gum-stained concrete at the base of a lamppost and leaned against his bags. Above him hummed a camera. Knees, ankles, hemlines hurried by. The tall man with the megaphone stood a few paces away, curiously motionless. Between the legs of the passing workers, the bagman struggled to read the front of the preacher's signboard. Written there, in green magic marker, were these words:

Why do you sleep, O Lord?
Why do you hide your face?

The preacher looked lost. He let the megaphone dangle at his thigh. His jaw hung slack. Pedestrians bumped him from all sides. He teetered, and fought to keep his balance. His chin twitched. One eye twitched, then his nose, and his cheekbones one by one. Each lip twitched, and each temple, each twitch a required step in a sequence of preparatory impulses necessary before some crucial internal circuit could be breached. Then a wave of determination overtook him. He placed himself squarely in the path of one man, and then another. They pushed him casually aside as if bending back a branch that hung too low over the trail in front of them. Undiscouraged, he held the megaphone to his mouth. A peal of feedback screeched from it. The crowd flinched, like fish do when a shadow passes over the surface of their pond. The man bent his lips into words, but no sound came forth. At last he stuttered, "H-h-h-h-h-h-h-how, h-h-how long?" He gazed deliberately around him as if expecting an answer to his query, but no one save the bagman and the cameras mounted high on the lampposts so much as glanced his way.

The preacher let the megaphone drop to his side. A strand of red hair unglued itself from his scalp and dangled over the earpiece of his glasses. His body slackened, as if some vital quality had been emptied from him. He let himself be jostled, and almost fell. Then once again, twitching overcame his features and he was suddenly renewed. He set his feet firmly apart. He squared his shoulders and filled his lungs with air. The lenses around his neck clattered into place. With booming conviction and without a moment's stutter, he declared, "He walks among us!" But he forgot to use the megaphone. The clatter of heels on the pavement and the screeching of the traffic swallowed his voice entirely. He remembered the thing in his fist and lifted it again to his lips. It was too late. All he could get out was another stammered "H-h-h-h-he . . ." before his enthusiasm again abandoned him.

The bagman sat among his bags like a giant, begrimed ceramic Buddha. He watched the stuttering preacher with great and growing interest. The crowds around them at last began to thin. The commuters' pace appeared to vary inversely in relation to the density of the crowds. The fewer there were, the more they hurried, as if solitude were a substance to be fled, a swarming pathogen, some noxious gas. The final few raced along the sidewalk, briefcases flapping like strange vestigial wings. Then they too disappeared around corners and through tall revolving doors.

At last the sidewalk was empty, the street free of cars. The preacher stood alone on the corner. His face was gray. Beneath the sandwich board, his tie hung limp. His shirt was drenched in sweat. He wrinkled his nose, as if noticing for the first time the odor hovering around the lamppost, radiating from the bearded man who sat beneath it. The preacher's eyes met the bagman's. One cheekbone twitched. He shook his head. He waved the megaphone, his gesture encompassing not only the bricks of the buildings, the gleaming windows, the chain of green lights that stretched on down the avenue, but also the crowds of people who were no longer there, and all the motivation for their haste. "N-n-n-none of it," the preacher said, defeated, "N-n-none of this is real."

The bagman nodded. He was cautious: the preacher's words could mean a lot of things. For instance, that though the particular shop windows and concrete curbs and squat blue mailboxes that surrounded them lacked real-ness, this failure was accidental, local, temporary, and other things in other places did possess that quality. Or that the matutinal haste and ant-like purposefulness of the gainfully employed was motivated by naught but stacked illusions. Or, solipsistically, that the preacher's experience of his own consciousness was somehow more real, more substantial and valid and true than anything he perceived in his immediate surroundings. But it was also possible, the bagman realized, that he had found someone who shared his root ontological mistrust. So the bagman took a risk. He spoke. He sucked a breath in through his nostrils, knit his brow and pursed his lips as if the effort of speech required a full gathering of the resources scattered about his face.

"What do you mean?" he asked.

"It's l-like so much," the preacher began, but then his tongue failed him and he almost had to spit to get the word out, "s-s-s-s-sand." He held out his free hand and spread its fingers wide.

"It falls right through," the bagman said.

The preacher nodded furiously. His glasses bounced on the bridge of his nose. The camera lenses clacked.

"Like steam," the bagman added, waving his own hand through the air.

"Y-yes," the preacher managed. "Like shit!"

The bagman paused and swallowed hard. He scratched himself, raised his eyebrows, dropped them down. "I've seen him," he said.

The preacher frowned. "Who?" he asked.

"Him."

"H-h-how do you know th-that it's him?"

The bagman crossed and uncrossed his legs. He indicated the bags behind him. "These belong to him."

The preacher's blue eyes opened wide behind the thick lenses of his glasses. He looked at the bags, then at the bagman, and considered what he saw. "Where d-d-did you see him? Wh-wh-wh-where is he?"

The bagman stood, straightening his trousers. "Saw him on the bus. Here. Near here. He left this morning. Can't have gone too far."

A full course of twitching ran across the preacher's chiseled face and down over the lumps of his throat. He asked the bagman which way, and the bagman pointed in the direction from which he had come. The preacher chewed his tongue. He smoothed his hair against his scalp. "I'm going to b-believe you," he said, and then got rolling and raced hungrily from word to word, unsure how long he had, when the capacity for speech would desert him. "Y-y-you better not be bullshitting me," he said, "I have no time for b-bullshit, no time for slacking off. I do things right or I d-don't do them and I do them all the way. I'm n-nobody's patsy and nobody's fool. So don't t-try and kiss me or slobber all over me and don't p-p-put your hand on my upper leg, on my thigh or on my hip or my b-b-b-buttock, and think I'll just leave it there. I don't need a backrub at any time. I know which path is right and w-w-which is wrong. I'm here for one reason and one reason only and no one's gonna keep me from it, so y-you got to act right. Consider yourself on p-p-probation, buster, consider yourself warned, no s-s-s-second chances, you g-g-got to c-carry your own weight around here." Then without another stuttered syllable, the preacher twirled on his heel.

The bagman regarded his bags ruefully and hoisted them again onto his back. The preacher, already ten paces ahead of him, walked with loping strides down the deserted street. The megaphone dangled on a strap from his bony wrist. Jogging to catch up, the bagman could just make out the words on the back of the sandwich board. They were written by hand in cramped cursive letters with a purple marker:

> Praise God in his sanctuary; praise him in his mighty
> firmament!
> Praise him with trumpet sound; praise him with lute and
> harp!
> Praise him with tambourine and dance!
> Let everything that breathes praise the Lord!

He drops in on a friend.

The subdivision crouched at the very peak of the highest hill around, but when he at last limped his way to the gate, the stranger was not winded. A stone wall had been built to protect the development from whatever evils lurked in the valley below, or at least to signify protection — it was too low to do much good. The guard shack at the entrance was abandoned, its windows coated with grime, and the gate itself, apparently once automated, had been derailed from its track. It lay rusting in the gravel. Only the camera affixed to the guard shack appeared to still be working. The stranger stepped past it, over the gate and into the curving streets. The houses were identical to one another, or nearly so, differentiated only by the varying strategies by which age and disrepair had conspired to render them unique. The red tile roofs were more and less intact. Some houses had been repainted, in whole or in part. Some had faded uniformly, while others did so in streaks, depending which side faced sun and which faced wind and rain. Most of the lawns had reverted to sand, but some here and there were better tended, and a few had been paved over, or strewn evenly with small white stones.

The streets were empty. No cars drove by. No kids rode bikes. No one walked dogs or toddlers. The stranger did not spot a single soul until he came across a car parked at an odd angle to the curb, idling, blocking a driveway. In the front seat sat two teenage girls. Through the windshield, he watched as one kissed the other's neck, hands tangled in her shortly cropped hair, rushing across her arms and breasts, clumsy with hunger. The eyes of the girl being kissed were closed. Her face was flushed, and a tear ran down her cheek. The stranger paused in front of the car. He took one step closer to the driver's side door, and then another. His left eye ticced as he fingered the twine that bound his package. He untied it. The girl being kissed opened her eyes, saw him standing there, and pushed her lover from her. They looked at the stranger — whose hand had disappeared beneath the brown paper wrapping his parcel — and then at one another. The girls blushed and laughed, unaware of any danger. The short-haired girl dried her cheek with her wrist. "Cheap thrills," she said without conviction to the stranger outside, "huh mister?" Then the one with longer hair put the car in drive, and they sped away.

The stranger stood for a moment, his eye still ticcing. He reknotted the twine and limped on along the sidewalk. He crossed the asphalt on a diagonal. He turned one corner and then another before arriving at last at a wide cul-de-sac. In the front yard of the third house, a tall balding man pushed an electric lawnmower, bending now and again to keep from running over the orange power cord. He wore headphones, rimless glasses, faded cargo shorts, an undershirt. His work was easy, as the yard was mainly dirt.

The house looked no better or worse than any of the others around, except for the black convertible sulking in the driveway, its top down, its paint immaculate. The stranger took a seat on the hood of the car, crossed his legs, and laid his package down beside him.

The balding man pivoted the mower on one rear wheel and swiveled round to trim another row of sand. "Hello Michael," the stranger said. "Impressive automobile."

Michael stopped. His face, flushed from the heat and the

mild exertion required by his task, paled. He cut the power on the mower and hit the stop button on the tape player hooked to his belt.

"I said, 'Nice ride,'" the stranger said.

Michael pulled the headphones from his ears, fumbled them, and let them dangle at his ankles by their cord. "How did you find me?" he coughed.

"Michael," the stranger clucked, grinning wide and tilting his head to one side. "Don't insult me."

Michael didn't smile back. "Please don't sit on the car," he said.

The stranger contorted his face, twisting his lips, his voice artificially high: "*Pleasedontsitonthecar.*" He didn't move. He sighed. "I've come a long way to see you, Michael. Why don't you offer me a drink. A nice cold soda pop."

Michael shook his head. "You can't go in the house. There's a hose around the side if you're thirsty."

The stranger scoffed. "A hose around the side? Why do you hurt me, Michael?"

"Why did you come here?"

The stranger smiled with exaggerated pain and lowered his eyes. "I hear you're in school," he said.

Michael nodded. "I finish in May," he said. "You can't stay here."

"And that you have a lovely wife."

"She's not here. And you can't meet her."

The stranger shook his head again. He rapped the windshield with his knuckles. "And such a handsome vehicle."

"A wedding present. My father-in-law. Please get off it now."

The stranger did not move. Instead he pointed to Michael's cassette player. "What were you listening to?" he asked.

"Bar review," answered Michael, blushing.

The stranger nodded. "Very nice. Bar review. What a delightful little life you have."

"I like it," Michael said.

"Of course you do."

The two of them regarded one another — Michael, standing stiff before his mower, still gripping its handle, the stranger seated on the convertible's hood, his legs crossed and his arms crossed too, his thumb pressed against his chin, peering at Michael with one brow cocked above the other.

Michael spoke. "I don't want you here."

The stranger laughed, a harsh little rumble from deep in his gut. "You've made that clear," he said. "I'm not going to try to convince you that I could give you so much more than this, whatever *this* is that you've settled for, that you've chosen to aspire to. That would not be worth my while. I wonder though — does she know, your wife? Does she know what you once had? Have you told her all the things you used to do? Does she worry that she can't compete with such a past? The poor thing is probably scared to death that you'll get bored of her, that you'll just up and leave this dusty little house one day. Because she must know how easy it would be for you to pick up where you left off, after a little effort anyway. Because it would be easy, Michael. We could have it all again. She must be really something, that little gal of yours. Or maybe it's the car that holds you back."

"What's in the package?"

The stranger was silent for a moment. "I think you know," he answered. "But what was I saying? Oh yes, your car. And your degree. You've worked so hard. Law, was it? Brilliant. Such delicate things, laws. Like little origami doves. Those ones about parking and whatnot, so interesting, have you learned those already? Or are those just regulations? Oh well, you'll shine, I'm sure. A nice office somewhere. A secretary. Free coffee all day long. Big windows, prestigious firm, a bonus if you bill enough hours. And maybe someday you'll make partner! How about that! Your name in polished brass. It's a fine metal, brass. I'm a little jealous. I'll bet a year from now you can afford to pay someone else to mow that lawn, some strapping neighborhood lad. Better keep an eye on the little lady, huh Michael? Watch out!"

The mockery dimmed in the stranger's eyes. His voice softened. "It's like I said. I'm not here to convince you I could give you anything better. I'm here for another reason, Michael. I'm here to remind you: You Made an Oath."

He hissed: "An oath, Michael, that binds you still."

For the first time since the stranger's arrival, Michael smiled. He tapped the mower's handle. "Do you remember if you wrote that down somewhere? That oath? I mean, did I sign anything? Because I don't remember that I did. That would make it an oral contract, which is fine, that's no less binding. It's just that without any witnesses, you might have a difficult case. Not to mention that a contract cannot be considered binding if it requires either party to convene the law in any way, or if it requires of either party any goods or services that they cannot be reasonably expected to provide. Remind me, what was the content of that oath you mentioned?"

The stranger smiled, patient. "You are not clever, Michael. You shouldn't try to be." He took a breath. "I am starting over. I will not make the same mistakes again. Come with me. Leave this behind. Or be left behind."

Michael tapped a finger against the mower's plastic grip. "And if I don't?"

"You know what I can do," the stranger said, and rested his palm on the package beside him.

Michael shook his head. "I know you won't."

The stranger's lip curled. "You don't know anything," he said.

Michael's glasses had steamed, and he wiped them on his shirt. He hit the power switch on the lawnmower and the play button on his cassette player. He retrieved his headphones and, his eyes on the task in front of him, commenced to mow the weeds and sand.

Sweetness.

The old woman's lower lip quivered in sleep. Her gray tongue darted in and out behind it like some blind and hungry rodent unconvinced of the benevolence of the world beyond its hole. And rightly so: the boy held a caterpillar between his pudgy, nailbit fingers. He let it hang just above his grandmother's lips. The caterpillar was brown and each segment of its back was intricately marked with an oval of red inside a black-bordered band of white inside another red oval. It had ceased wriggling hours ago, and swayed limply back and forth in time with the old woman's breathing and the to-and-fro-ing of her tongue. He lowered it until its black face just touched her fallen lower lip. The tongue shot out. He pulled the caterpillar quickly up and away from her face and began to put it in the pocket of his t-shirt. He thought better of it, and laid the caterpillar on her shoulder. It didn't move.

The old woman snorted and wiped her mouth with the back of her hand. Her clouded eyes blinked open, sightless though they were. "That boy," she muttered to herself. The boy, fat, with an uncertain, shifting gaze, tiptoed three long steps backwards.

"Sweetness," she croaked. "You home?"

"I'm right here grandma."

"Come here and give your grandmother a hand."

The boy helped the old woman to stand, his eyes on the caterpillar beside the collar of her blouse. "Where do you want to go?" he asked.

"Just point me at the kitchen and I'll be fine."

She counted her steps until she was standing in front of the small stove. On the third step, the caterpillar tumbled from her shoulder onto the floor. The boy leapt out and grabbed it, then ran with it into a back room. The old woman took the kettle from the burner to her left, filled it with water from the sink, and lit a match to ignite the gas. "You eaten yet?" she asked.

The boy reappeared at the edge of the linoleum that separated the kitchen from the small, uncarpeted living room. He held his hands cupped one over the other. He was panting slightly from his sprint across the house. "No, grandma," he said.

"Well fix yourself a sandwich if you're hungry. There's ham in the icebox. You know what to do."

The woman took four slow steps to her right and extended a hand until she felt the formica tabletop. She pulled a chair out, lowered herself into it and waited for the water to boil.

"You need anything, grandma?" asked the boy.

"You're very sweet," the old woman said. "Just bring me the teacup from the drainboard."

Closing his left fist with care, the boy placed a cup and saucer in front of the old woman. He fished a teabag from the box on the counter, and emptied his left hand over the cup, freeing a thumb-sized beetle. The bug lay on its back at the base of the cup, its feet scrambling for purchase on the air. The boy laid the teabag on top of it. "Are you gonna want cream?" he asked.

"Thank you. You know I will."

The boy pulled the carton from the door of the refrigerator, placed it on the table beside the sugarbowl, and took a seat behind his grandmother. He leaned forward to stare into the bottom of her teacup to watch the bug struggle to right itself.

"Do you have much homework?"

"No, grandma," the boy lied. "I did it on the bus."

The kettle whistled. "I'll get it," the boy said.

"You're a dear."

The boy stood beside his grandmother, the kettle steaming in his hand. The beetle's antennae slithered against the smooth white china. The teabag twitched above it as he watched. He returned the kettle to the stove, lifted the teabag and shook the insect back into his palm. Replacing the teabag, he poured hot water into the cup.

"What is it dear?" his grandmother asked.

"There was something in your cup."

The boy ran again into the back room. With the beetle wriggling against his palm, he covered the lens of the video camera on the wall with his ball cap and pulled a cookie tin from beneath the small sofa that served as his bed. It contained a pair of sewing scissors he'd stolen from his grandmother; an old bone-handled penknife that he liked to think had belonged to his father, though in fact he nicked it from another boy at school; a sealed plastic bottle of butane; a .22 cartridge he'd found in a field; a scallop shell and a disk of violet-colored beach glass he brought home from the shore years before; a black-and-white photograph of a young man in military dress; a yellow plastic cocktail sword that was the one thing he possessed that his mother had given him, originally impaled with three sweet cherries dripping bourbon; and seven red matchboxes, worn from overhandling. He removed the topmost matchbox and shook it to make sure that it was empty. He slid it open, shoved the beetle inside, and slid it closed. The matchbox beneath it contained four white grubs crammed against one another, none of them displaying any signs of life. The boy considered them for a moment — just this morning, they had been wriggling still — but a tap at the window distracted him.

"Tubs!" said a voice from outside, barely constrained to a whisper. "You coming out?"

His grandmother called from the kitchen. "Sweetness," she said.

The boy hastily closed the matchbox, put the penknife in his pocket, and shoved the tin back beneath the cushions. "What is it grandma?" he shouted.

"Tubs," the voice from outside called again. "We're leaving."

"I'd like you to read to me, dear," his grandmother said.

"*Read to me, Tubby,*" the voice outside mocked.

The boy grabbed his cap and scrambled back to the kitchen. "I gotta go now, grandma," he said. "I have practice." His fist was already on the doorknob.

"Oh," his grandmother answered. "Perhaps later then." But the boy had left the house. The screen door squeaked shut behind him.

The old woman sipped at her tea. On creaking knees, she raised herself from the table, took four steps to her left until she could feel the rim of the sink in front of her. She twisted the tap until the water ran warm, then rinsed the cup and saucer and returned them to the drainboard. "The man on the radio said it's going to rain," she announced to the empty room. "And it does feel like rain, don't you think?" She waited a moment for an answer. None came. She closed the tap, but the faucet still dripped, pinging every third second against the steel basin of the sink.

He raises the dead.

Muttering beneath his breath, the stranger stared at his feet as he walked beside the tracks. He kicked a rock in front of him. Gabriel and Michael had both refused him. How to start all over? To take hold of the world and the forces that bind it, that suture time to space, gravity to hunger to greed?

When he rounded a bend, the air grew suddenly rank, sharp and sweet with drifting rot. Instead of bouncing to a stop in the dirt, the rock the stranger had kicked thudded into something soft. It was green, bulky. A sleeve. The sleeve of an army jacket. An arm in the sleeve of an army jacket. The arm of a man lying on his face in the dirt, the neck of a broken bottle gripped in one gray hand.

The stranger stopped. He nudged the jacket with his foot. There was no give to the torso beneath it. The man had gone stiff. The stranger kicked him over on his back. The man's heart had long ceased pumping, and, with nowhere else to go and nothing much to do, his blood had drained down into his face. The red blood cells had all expired, and none kept their color long, so the face was clotted bluish black. On the brow above one eye a wound had been carved, perhaps by a lonely drunken stumble, perhaps by a blow from a bottle or a stick, a pair of brass knuckles, a railroad spike. No matter, it did what it did, whatever it was, leaving now an ugly open slit, dried and crusted with pebbles, leaves and grass.

The stranger drew himself up, his spine straight, his chin high. He kicked the corpse again. "Stand," he said.

But the corpse did not stand.

He kicked at the torso, where the ribs and beneath them the idle lungs and heart were hidden by the heavy jacket. "Rise," he said.

But the corpse did not rise.

He kicked at the blue-black head. His shoe and broken toe ripped through the corpse's cheek. "Rise!" the stranger said again.

But the corpse did not rise, again.

He pulled away his foot. The dead lips fell and curled into a mocking grimace. He ignored the pain in his own broken toe, and kicked at the head again, smearing the grin from its mouth with mud. He kept kicking, and when he had kicked enough, he commenced to stomp. He flattened the corpse's face, tore it in putrid pieces. With his heel he crushed the skull, and kept stomping until he had stomped it flat. He shattered the ribs and with them pierced the organs. He broke the spine, the pelvis and the hips. The stink worsened, and the stranger, panting, stopped. His breath ragged and quick, he untied his parcel, stepped back and aimed at the trampled remains.

In the time it takes to close one eye and open it again, all evidence of the stranger's fury was undone. The corpse pieced itself together, regained volume and integrity. The gelled blood drained from its face. The flesh turned back to pink. The wrinkles, furrows and scars were smoothed. The hair went from gray to brown and finally to tow-head blond, as the skin grew fresh again and bright and the bones shrank to child-size and finally it was a frightened boy who opened his eyes, lifted himself from the ground and stood. The stranger tried to reach out to him, to take his hand, but he wasn't fast enough by far, and the boy, arisen, shattered like a bottle toppled from a roof, not to shards but to dust that fell again to the earth, a sprinkling of dirt on dirt.

The stranger stood there for a moment, saddened and somehow calmed, then retied his bundle and moved on. The stink clung to his clothes.

I threaten him.

The stranger sits beside me on the couch. He leans forward, his elbows on his knees, his head cradled in his palms. A newspaper lies folded at his feet. He looks paler than usual. His lips are whiter than his beard. I can't see his eyes at all.

I point to the paper. "Is that today's?"

He doesn't answer.

"Are you reading it?" I ask.

He still ignores me, so I reach down and take the paper from him. But he's sitting in the middle of the couch and I just have this tiny corner here beside him, so I tell him to move over, but he doesn't acknowledge me and doesn't move at all. I elbow him a little, but it's like he's cast in bronze and welded to the cushions. I read the first page, skim the rest. It's not today's. I bought it yesterday and forgot it on the floor. My fingers smudge the headlines. The usual catalogue of horrors. A monsoon somewhere unpronounceable. Twelve thousand dead. An earthquake buries eight times more. These are estimates: the only people left to count are busy digging. A photo of a dusty leg. Something about a flood. Fires raging through slums. Bridge collapses. TV star gets drunk. Tidal wave. Ferry sinks with all aboard. Corpses ruin beaches, tourists complain. Aerial assault flattens ancient city. Again. The dead are dark and poor, oddly attired, too numerous to count. Sixty die in ambush. Line 'em up. Suicide bomb kills ninety-four as they kneel at worship. To whom should we pray now? survivor asks. Movie star is fatter than before. Tanks flatten village, house by crumbling house. Headless toddler declares self non-combatant. President auto-fellates and toasts to human misery. Husband cheats on wife. Man in fancy car farts, gets paid. Rain falls on the fields of the rich. Blame the starving that they have not to eat. Cop declares torture fun. These are fine lines, pundits agree. Is it genocide or just mass murder? Build more walls, public demands. A new vision for the nation: A cage for every soul. Race-sickness transmitted through blood and blood alone. But we all have blood, sighs expert. Don't panic, government advises: Famine kills only the hungry. Superstar actor swears fealty to humanitarian ideals. This world of washboard ribs, rheumy eyes, lies and lies, sick pussing lies.

I throw the paper on the floor, kick it away, try to crumple it with my heel. But newspapers are unwieldy beasts. It won't fight back, but it flaps open again, spreads itself wantonly at my feet. I kick at it again and rest my elbows on my knees. I cradle my head in my hands. The newsprint rustles lewd whispers at my toes. The stranger looks up at me and laughs.

"Nothing's funny," I say.

He chuckles, cracking the knuckles on his right hand one by one. "I know," he says.

"Is that all you have to say?" I ask him.

"To say?"

I nod toward the paper. "To say. For all of this."

He doesn't answer at first, just sits there and stares at me, his eyes dripping slow contempt. At last he speaks. "You're being childish. You don't really mean to blame me?"

"Who else?" I ask.

He smiles, almost politely, but doesn't answer. I didn't mean to, but I think I may have flattered him.

"Move over," I tell him, and elbow him again.

"No."

"I'll get you."

The stranger snorts and feigns a yawn. He doesn't move at all.

"I will," I say. "Just watch."

He encounters a setback.

Barely a hundred yards down the tracks from where the corpse had lain, three men stepped out from the bushes, buttoning their trousers. Behind the bushes was an old tin-roofed railroad shack, and the men had just finished painting it with their urine, which coursed down one wall in terraced stains at different heights. For though the men all three had shaved heads and all wore black dungarees, black nylon bomber jackets and shiny boots with thick, red laces, they were of markedly different statures. One was tall and skinny, another tall and fat, and the third was short and fat. They blocked the stranger's path.

"Looky looky," said the tall and skinny.

"What have we here?" said the tall and fat.

The short and fat said nothing, but only cracked his knuckles, scratched himself and spat.

"Good afternoon," said the stranger to the men.

"Afternoon?" snickered the tall and fat. "He thinks it's afternoon."

"Afternoon!" echoed the tall and skinny with a guffaw.

The short and fat fished a silver pocket watch from the pocket of his jeans. "It's three p.m.," he said.

The tall and skinny flexed his brow, impressed. "Good afternoon," he said, and bowed.

The tall and fat stepped forward. "This afternoon there is a toll."

"A toll?" the stranger said.

"No," said the tall and skinny. "Not a mole. A toll. You have to pay to pass."

"And what is the toll this afternoon?" the stranger inquired, a grin spreading across his face.

"No, no," said the short and fat, cracking the knuckles of his right hand. "A vole is a small, defenseless critter, blind and hairless, like a mole but with a *v*. There is no vole this afternoon. And no mole. You can't get out of this so easy. There is a toll. You have to pay."

"Yes," the stranger said, loosening the binding of his package. "I understand. But *what* do you want me to pay?"

"This is a thick one," the tall and fat sighed to his companions, shaking his head in disbelief. "No one said a word about a ray. A ray is like a fish, but flatter, and with a spiky sort of tail. The point is, smart boy, you have to pay."

"He didn't say ray," chuckled the tall and thin. "He called you gay."

"He did not call me gay," answered the tall and fat, stepping forward to grab a twist of the stranger's shirt in his fist and lifting him by it so that his shoes dangled just above the dirt. "He's not dumb. He's just confused." He shook the stranger slightly. "He'll straighten out."

"Listen," said the stranger, his voice calm despite his newly precarious position. "Perhaps we can help each other. How would you boys like to be of some use?"

"Did he say what I thought he said?" asked the tall and thin.

"He couldn't have," said the short and fat.

"He did," said the tall and fat, excited. "I heard him clear. He called us Jews."

The tall and fat closed his free hand into a fist as large as the stranger's head, and with it pounded him hard in the face.

When the stranger's head snapped back, the tall and fat hit him again. The stranger's body slackened. His package dropped from beneath his arm. The tall and fat opened his other fist, and when the stranger crumpled to the ground, all three fell upon him, a stomping storm of red-laced black boots, harder than they looked, tall and short and fat and skinny, digging into ribs and skull and gut.

When the stranger regained consciousness, the three men were a quarter mile down the tracks. He could just barely hear them singing, and could see them silhouetted against the white sky, tossing something merrily between them: a package. His. He let his head fall back into the dirt, and did not open his eyes again that day.

The ether.

In the lots that sprawled at the edge of the city, not far from the underpass where the bagman and the stranger had together passed a night, the bagman and the preacher came across another man. High reeds grew out of the broken concrete and shattered glass, and swallows dove among them. The man's back was to them. He was an old man, white-haired, bent at the waist, all sagging flesh and brittle bone. He walked as if he were carrying a cane, though he had none. And he spoke as if he had an audience, declaiming loudly and enunciating with great care, though he showed no sign that he was aware that two men had paused behind him.

"Above the clouds there are other clouds," the old man said, and jabbed a crooked finger at the sky. "They are whiter than these ones, and softer, and above them is the sun. Between the sun and this second tier of clouds is the ether. They don't have elevators to get there. You can't take a plane. This is the ether, people." The old man kicked a rusted beer can to accentuate his point. "That's why they call it ethereal. Up there, there are no bugs or birds. There are no angels flying around. It's thinner than all that. Bugs can't even breathe in the ether. It's pure. It's clean. It's pure of living things. Only ghosts can live up there. That's where things go when they're done being what they were, and things that never were, but might have been. It's not heaven. It's no dreamland — this is science, people. This is physics. Matter cannot be created or destroyed, it can only change its form. So where does it go? What form does matter take when it's not matter anymore? Where did Mount Saint Helen go?"

The old man paused in his oration to sniff at the air. He'd caught the bagman's scent. He turned around and saw them standing there: the fat, dingy-bearded man, his grimy belly hanging out from under a grimier reindeer sweater, a tall, skinny man almost swallowed by the sandwich board he wore, and three stuffed bags behind them. The old man winked at his watchers, and went on, "There was a whole mountain there, a big one. We all saw it. Not any more. It's not there. Matter cannot be created or destroyed. It can only change form. I have seen so much. So many things I can't account for. Where did my wife go? What form is she taking? Once upon a time I intended to become a highly paid shortstop in the major leagues. Where is the man I meant to be? What happened to the Union of Soviet Socialist Republics? The stains I've left on the sheets of the world, hundreds of sheets, thousands of stains — where did they go? Where is the soap that washed them? Where does the soul go when the body dies? Where did your momma go? Where does the stinking body go? Where did the love go, people? Shit, it all becomes a ghost."

The old man hobbled over, smiling slyly, pleased with his performance. The bagman greeted him with a nod and hoisted up his bags. The preacher resumed walking. The old man fell in with them. Despite his age and his broken gait, he had no trouble keeping up, and talked as he walked beside them.

"I worked at the dog track over there," the old man said. "You'll pass it up ahead. Twenty-six years. I did every job there was to do. When the track closed — it was at least ten years ago, I'm not counting — but when it closed they told me and another fellow to take care of the dogs. I mean kill them. The other fellow had a little .38 and we took turns shooting them.

114

They were half-starved so it did feel more like mercy than meanness. When we ran out of bullets we crushed their skulls with shovels. Greyhounds aren't pit bulls. They're delicate dogs. Their heads aren't that hard, but still they could take a few good whacks, some of them could. Nothing likes to die. It took hardly an hour to finish them all. I've done worse things than that in my life but nothing's ever made me feel so bad."

The old man studied the words written on the preacher's signboards. "Why do you hide your face?" he read aloud and laughed. "If only he did hide it. I've seen it enough. Ugly old bastard."

The preacher shot the old man a hard look. His nose flinched and his blue eyes flinched and he seemed to be about to say something, but he didn't. The bagman did. "Where did you see it?" he asked. "His face?"

The old man inserted an index finger into one ear and twisted it about. "Let me put it to you this way," he said, frowning as he inspected the harvest on the tip of his finger. "Nowhere nice."

He grinned and switched ears. "Where you fellows off to, you mind if I ask?"

The preacher and the bagman looked at one another for a long moment, as if trying to decide which one could speak with the least effort, or if they should speak at all. At last the bagman answered. "We're looking for him," he said.

"Him?"

"I saw him," the bagman nodded. "We're gonna find him."

The old man twisted his face to one side and then the other. "Him, huh?" he said. "What do you want to find him for?"

The preacher turned and regarded the old man with his best

115

schoolmaster's sneer. But the old man would not be shamed. He winked at the preacher. "Seek and ye shall find," he said. "Ain't that how it goes? Ask and ye shall receive. Merrily merrily merrily merrily, gently down the stream. Something like that right? That's a funny necklace. You make it yourself?"

The old man did not wait for an answer, but went on: "Satan, Jesus and Mohammed walked into a bar, you know that one? Satan was wearing a backpack, stuffed full. Jesus had two Jews in a cigarette box in his shirt pocket and Mohammed had a Buddhist sitting on each shoulder, meditating like they do, Indian style. The bartender's standing there drying glasses when they all come in and he puts down his bar-rag, grabs the bat he keeps beneath the bar and says . . ."

The old man stopped mid-joke. "You two are serious, aren't you?"

The bagman shook his head, then nodded, correcting himself.

The old man spat. He kicked dirt over his spittle. He twisted his face again, then untwisted it halfway. "You think you can just wander about and find him. Like he's a golden retriever escaped his leash. Like maybe he just went to the library, will be back in time for lunch. Pizza!" He tried to spit again but his mouth was dry, so he made a thin, hocking sound and said, "Shit. I've done stupider things."

The three walked on. The old man's mood improved. He finished his joke and told another about Saint Francis making love to twin canaries and a third about a blind priest seduced by his own colostomy bag. They skirted the sand pits and the truck yards. They passed the dog track and the old man fell silent. Without noticing it, the old man stepped on a praying mantis and smashed the only thorax its creator had thought to give it. The preacher's black sneaker crushed an anthill, killing or crippling two dozen scrambling insects and undoing the labor of a thousand more. A mosquito drained blood from the folds of flesh beneath the bagman's ankle. A toad ate the mosquito, and grew fat off the bagman's blood. The old man whistled a melancholy tune. The wind accompanied him, sissing through the grass.

They surprised a little, brown-skinned boy dashing across the tracks. The boy stopped like a deer caught out in the open. He stared at them. They were, they realized, a minor spectacle. The preacher stuttered for a while, but it was the bagman who ultimately got out the words. He asked the boy if he had seen a tall man in a white suit pass by, holding a package wrapped in brown paper beneath his arm. The boy didn't answer, but ran off, head bobbing as he disappeared into the brush.

"You sure you ain't seen him?" the old man yelled after the boy. "He's seen him. Maybe didn't like him any more than he liked seeing us, but he seen him. 'Suffer the little children,' doesn't it say that in your book?" he said, elbowing the preacher. "That's the eleventh commandment, ain't it? Make sure the little fuckers suffer good."

The preacher stuttered out a flustered "no," and marched off, showing the old man his back and the edict that it bore: "Let everything that breathes praise the Lord."

Slow, in single file, the men walked on beneath low, gray clouds. Above those floated other clouds, whiter and softer than those immediately overhead. Above them was the sun, above it the stars. Above them were other stars and more stars still and all the hungry space that connects one star to another and that holds them at the same time apart. And somewhere up there in the space between the spaces, and in the spaces between those, if you searched hard enough you'd find them: barking dogs and fallen mountains, the praying mantis, all the ants.

And another.

When he at last awoke, the stranger was no longer lying in the dirt where he had fallen, but in a small, dark room with a floor of cracked concrete. Rain beat hard on the metal roof. The floor was damp, as was the stranger's suit. The room reeked of urine and of mold. The stranger's ankles had been tied together, and his wrists were bound behind him, so he could not remove whatever warm, soft thing it was that filled his mouth. He tried to spit it out, but was unable. He gagged, and tried to choke it out, but that also did not work. He twisted his hands and tried to wriggle out of the ropes that bound him, but he could not do that either.

He heard rustling nearby, steps somewhere outside. He moaned as loud as he could with his mouth obstructed, and banged his feet against the floor. Behind him, a door opened. Light poured in. Rain came with it at a diagonal through the door. Standing above him were the four boys who had stoned him the day before. All four wore yellow slickers. They removed their hoods, shook rain onto the floor.

"Take the mouse out," the first boy said.

"You take it out," said the second.

"I'm not touching that thing," said the fourth boy. "It's slimy."

"Yeah," agreed the second. "And he's awake now. He might bite."

"He might yell," the third boy added.

"Let's cut off his fingers," said the fourth boy, the fat one.

"What for?" asked the first.

"We could each take three," the fat boy answered.

"No, stupid," said the second boy. "Then he'd have to have 15 fingers."

"Fine," said the fat boy. "We'll each take four."

"That's smart," the first boy said. "Then his prints would get all over. That's how you get caught."

"I want to cut off his ear," the third boy said.

"Cut off his thing!" enthused the fourth boy.

"You're a faggot," said the third.

"Why do you guys want to cut stuff off him?" the first boy asked.

The fourth boy shrugged. "That way we won't forget. So we'll all be friends forever."

The boys were briefly silent, taking in this thought.

"It's not gonna look good," the first boy cautioned. "It's only gonna rot."

"No, it won't," objected the fourth.

"It's meat, stupid. It rots."

Before they could fully contemplate that notion, and bring their discourse to any resolution, the stranger, ignoring the pain in his fractured ribs and damaged kidneys, focused all his strength on his diaphragm and in one great burst expelled the mouse from his mouth. It skidded to a stop about two feet from his head, its fur matted, half crushed. The stranger coughed and spat a black lump of blood onto the ground in front of him.

"Put the mouse back in!" the first boy squealed.

"You!" whined the second.

"Stuff it in his bum," chimed the fourth.

"Faggot!" screamed the other three.

The stranger spat again and cleared his throat. "Hello boys," he croaked. "Untie me."

"His eyes are freaky," the second boy said.

"I can help you," coughed the stranger, struggling with the rope that bound his wrists. "I can give you anything you want. I can make you into men, into something stronger still."

"He's a perv," the third boy said.

"How you gonna help us if you can't even untie your own hands?" the first boy asked.

"Untie me," the stranger said. "And I will show you how."

"We're gonna be late for soccer," said the second boy.

"There's no soccer today," said the fourth. "It's raining, dip-shit."

"You'll never have a chance like this again," the stranger said.

"There's practice inside, asshole," the second boy said. "In the gym."

"Yeah," the third boy said. "Let's go. He'll be here when we get back." They put on their hoods and zipped their slickers.

"Boys," the stranger said. "Untie me. I'll make it worth your while."

The first boy picked the mouse up by the tail. "Just hold his mouth open," he said. "Can you pussies at least do that?"

The dog again.

The dog was sleeping in the road again. The long-haired girl stopped the car in front of it. The wide bench seat beside her was empty. The back seat too. She was close enough to see the dog's eyelids flutter and its dry black nostrils swell with every breath. She shook a cigarette from her pack and pushed in the lighter on the dash.

The short-haired girl had met a boy and declared their friendship suspended. For now at least, she'd said. The short-haired girl had cried. The long-haired girl, her former friend, had not. The short-haired girl's nose had run. She had blubbered. I'm so confused, she'd said. The long-haired girl said nothing. But when she later saw the short-haired girl kissing the boy in the hall, it had made her feel as if her ribs had snapped inside her chest, as if their jagged ends were scraping against her lungs. She could still feel them scrape. The lighter popped. She pulled it from the dash and pushed its glowing end against her cigarette. She took a long drag, and coughed. Her foot trembled on the brake.

The heat from the engine caused the air above the hood to quiver. The dog let out a small yelp in its sleep, chasing dream rabbits down dream holes and across wide, dream-rabbity fields. Its lip flapped and exposed its yellow teeth and the mottled pink and black of its gums. It was an old dog. Its skin hung from its bones like a separate creature, imperfectly attached. The long-haired girl suddenly hated the dog, its passivity, its sleep. If she were just to lift her foot from the brake pedal, she would not even have to turn the wheel to run square over its head.

She looked in the rear-view mirror. There was no one behind her and no one in front. But the creepy guy who lived across the street to her left stood in his driveway, hosing soap from a shiny, black convertible Saab. He wore headphones, and was glaring at her. She glared back. "What?" she said, flicking her ash out the window as she turned the wheel, released the brake, and steered around the dog.

She drove out past the gate, dropped the shifter into neutral and rode the brakes all the way down the hill. She drove aimlessly, turning when she felt like turning. She drove into neighborhoods her parents had warned her to avoid, down empty blocks lined with liquor stores and churches with hand-painted signs. Men and women pushed shopping carts listlessly down the sidewalks, their baskets stuffed with plastic bags. She rolled up her window and locked the doors, then mocked herself for doing so, and unrolled the window and unlocked the doors. She flicked her cigarette butt into the street. Stopped at a light, she watched a policeman point his gun at four teenage boys with hands held high above their heads while another policeman berated them, red-faced and demonic. She locked her door again.

Three blocks later two more policemen had handcuffed a man beside his shopping cart and with gloved hands were tossing his bags into the street. She stopped the car and looked on through the window until the handcuffed man caught her eye and she saw something like hatred boiling in his gaze and she felt suddenly ashamed and understood that just by witnessing it, she had become complicit in his humiliation. She dropped her eyes, and drove on.

She drove into the depths of the city. The streets were

crowded, but no one was looking at anyone else. No one was holding hands or walking arm in arm. Music blared from other cars and out of storefronts, their bright windows lined with naked mannequins. She ran a red light and checked her mirror for police cars. After that she drove too cautiously, causing other drivers to honk and curse her when she failed to obey a green light with appropriate enthusiasm.

She wished she had a radio. She knew another cigarette would make her gag, but she pushed in the lighter on the dash again anyway because she enjoyed waiting for it to pop out — something small to hope for. She inhaled deeply and didn't gag. She turned and found the freeway and drove out again, back into the smooth-paved suburban wastes where no music played and no one walked the streets.

The long-haired girl slowed to observe a small procession of men advancing in single file down the graveled curb. Their leader wore a sandwich board and a necklace of black-rimmed lenses. A megaphone trailed from a strap on his wrist. Behind him walked a bent old man, and behind him rolled twin cripples in matching wheelchairs. Holding up the rear was a fat man dragging three stuffed lawn and leaf bags. One of the cripples waved to her. She waved back and drove on.

The orange Empty light flashed on the dash. "Shit," the long-haired girl cursed aloud. She had no money to buy gas. She turned the car around to face the direction she thought might be home. She drove over a bottle. It popped beneath the tire and she cursed again. Her anger flared. She wanted the short-haired girl to hurt as she did, in exactly the same spot. She wanted a hole to open in her rib cage and close only when she bade it close. She wanted boils to erupt on every patch of flesh she had been foolish enough to kiss. She wanted the traces of her saliva to morph to toxic sap. She wanted the short-haired girl's hair to fall out where she had gently tugged it. She punched the steering wheel. Why couldn't the world outside better resemble the one she felt inside? Why couldn't everything be in flames?

He escapes.

The stranger waited until he could no longer hear the boys crashing through the bushes. He lay on the concrete floor and listened to the echoes of the raindrops on the roof. It was so loud that he thought the rain was falling inside his head, another downpour of kicks and blows. After a few minutes had passed, he rolled onto his back and over again until his hands were aligned with the edge of the door. He slid his legs beneath him, then with his back to the wall he pushed himself up, catching at the knob with his hands. He turned it behind him, leaned on the door, and swung himself out into the rain.

The stranger stood outside the same railroad shack on the wall of which his assailants had earlier been pissing. Two small windows were boarded up, from within and from without, but the plywood outside one had been torn off, leaving a long crescent shard of pane which caught the stranger's image. His hair lay flat against his head, matted and dark with blood. His face, normally gaunt, was swollen, his nose broken and twisted twice its normal size. His right cheek was crudded up with mud and pocked with tiny gashes from being stomped against the rocks. He was bleeding from a tear across his forehead, and more blood had crusted down beneath his nostrils. His beard was as befilthed as his face and hair, and from between his lips swayed the stiff black tail of a mouse.

He did not look into his eyes, but tore himself away from the shack, and hopped off into the rain. He hopped from puddle to puddle and made it almost half a mile before his legs gave out and he toppled face forward into the mud.

I clear my throat, again.

I wake to find the stranger standing beside the bed. That's not quite right. I'm not sleeping, and if you're not sleeping it's hard to wake. But my eyes are closed, and she's asleep beside me, her head on my shoulder, her palm resting on my chest. I count my breaths until I lose track and I start over and begin counting again until it bores me and after that I stop and just lie there listening to her slow breathing and to the rain beating against the windows and the aluminum gutters and the roof and when I open my eyes I see him looming above me, a shadow among shadows. He's dripping all over the floor.

The stranger's voice is ragged. "Are you going to tell me anything?" he says.

I put one finger to my lips. I lift her hand from my chest and her head from my shoulder. I slide out from beneath her, kiss her sleeping eyelids, and point him to the door.

We walk out through the darkened living room to the porch. He leaves a thin trail of mud on the floor behind him. My feet are bare, and with every step I feel the cold, wet grit of the tracks he's left. His gait is cramped and painful, his limp worse than before. He trips over the carpet, bangs his shin on the coffee table, curses.

"Quiet," I hiss.

I unbolt the door and step out onto the porch behind him. In the yellow light of the streetlamps I can see that his face is a mess, bloated with bruises, marked here and there by clotted cuts as if some overeager illiterate had tried to carve a word into his face. Mud is the only thing holding his suit together.

He sits first, lets himself fall into the chair. He hugs his chest and shivers. Out on the boulevard at the bottom of the hill a drunk is yelling and a dog is barking at the drunk. The rain is fine and not as heavy as before. The air feels thin somehow, as if the world were quietly expanding, as if things were stretching farther and farther apart in increments too small to be observed. Which they are. The stranger curls his lip.

"What's so important?" I ask him.

Spacing the words for emphasis, or perhaps from fatigue, he repeats his question: "Are you going to tell me anything?"

I smile, shake my head. "I'm tired," I tell him. "The rain used to help me sleep, but it doesn't lately. It used to knock me right out, the pitter patter of it. Like those tapes people buy to help them relax so that they can uncover their hidden potential, get promotions and whatnot, do good in school."

He interrupts, "Are you going to *tell* me anything?"

A bird wakes up a block away and sings despite the drizzle. Or maybe it's a car alarm. "That's all I've been doing," I say. "You just don't notice. You don't notice anything."

He tries to laugh but it sounds more like he's swallowed something wrong. "So I should thank you," he says. "All of this is for my benefit. For my betterment."

"No," I tell him. "Don't flatter yourself. It's not about you anymore."

He laughs for real this time, a strange, broken, falsetto chortle, like someone whistling through a sieve. He's hugging his ribs and I can tell that each convulsion hurts him.

"I'll tell you a story if you'd like."

"Aren't you doing that already?" he asks.

"Fine. I'll tell you a joke instead. This priest gets colitis.

It's awful, diarrhea all the time, blood and mucus in the stool, constant pain. He tries everything, special all-broccoli diets, steroids, fasting, disgusting herbal remedies, acupuncture, yoga, everything, then finally the doctor tells him he has no other options, he'll have to have his colon surgically removed."

The stranger groans. He looks so awful sitting there, dripping, that I almost feel bad for him. "Okay," I say. "Forget the priest. I'll tell you the story."

"Just tell me how it ends," he says.

"Don't be silly," I tell him. "Nothing ends. Now listen." I clear my throat, and I tell this story:

"Once upon a time there was a little boy. He was never born, but was always a little boy. It never occurred to him that he should regret this — who remembers his own birth, much less what came before it? The little boy was lonely, though, as we all are lonely. That he did regret. To shake off the grasp of solitude, he taught himself to build things. He built castles out of young, green twigs, cities out of chewing gum, bottle glass and sand, whole planets out of fish scales, clay and rubber bands. He tossed his planets in the air sequentially and blew at them one by one out of the corner of his mouth until they spun in wide ellipses round his head."

The stranger interrupts me. "So I'm this little boy?" he asks.

"No," I tell him. "You're not a little boy. You're a scared old man. Now listen.

"The little boy felt no less alone for all his tricks, so he undertook to build himself a friend. He collected the feathers that he found stuck beneath tangled, reaching tree roots or caught shivering in the tall reeds around ponds. He stretched the feathers into wings. He balled rubber cement between his palms to form a breast, two thighs, a head. He found a sharp, hinged seashell for a beak, two small black seeds for eyes. He built a bird.

"With his little boyish breath held tightly in his lungs, the little boy kissed the tiny feathers he had woven over the bird's rubber cement scalp. He giggled when it warmed his hands and shook itself to life. Delight flooded his eyes. But the bird flew away. He could not follow.

"Sadness curled the little boy's heart. The sky dimmed. The air grew cold. The plants ceased growing. Their leaves dried and fell to the ground around the little boy, who lay there in the dirt, his fingers still sticky with rubber cement, unable to convince himself to stand. For the length of a season, the little boy mourned the bird and the sun barely dared to show itself."

"I don't like this story," the stranger says.

"It's not over yet," I tell him, and go on. "Eventually the air warmed and the boy remembered the pleasure of the sun's heat on his limbs. He stood. He stretched. He even smiled at the clouds.

"The little boy decided to build himself a fish. He crafted fish bones out of twist ties and dental floss, filled them out with river mud, and stretched around it all a bolt of purple sequined cloth. For eyes he used smooth pebbles he found along the shore, for gills the blue plastic heads of twin-bladed razors. He cut his thumb on one, and smeared the blood along the fish's belly. He held his breath and kissed its head. The fish wriggled between his palms. He laughed aloud. He ran to the shore, stripped to his shorts, and with the fish in one hand, dove into the sea. A wave knocked him over. The fish swam away. He held his breath and watched as it shimmied off into the blue.

"His sadness grew. To be lonely because you've always been alone is one thing. To be left behind is quite another. The earth grew cold again. The boy wept, and for a while everything that lived died or slept as if it had died. At last the boy dried his eyes and rose again, determined. Saplings grew, and flowers, and green shoots, and it was once again possible for the boy to imagine that he would not always be alone.

"He spread a piece of white carpet across a rock and filled it with toothpicks and wire and knotted thread. He made a rabbit. It hopped away. With a soggy towel, umbrella spines and shards of broken crockery he built a dog. It jumped from his arms. He grabbed its tail. It bit his fingers and ran off. He built a little girl out of blender blades, soft bread, green moss, and styrofoam. He stroked her rayon eyelids and kissed her beachglass eyes. She took one quick and hungry breath, then kissed him back. Then she pushed him to the ground and skipped away, singing to herself. By the time he had brushed himself off to give chase, the little girl was gone.

"Sometimes, in the long night that followed her departure, the little boy thought he heard her voice again, her weird, word-less song. He could feel her rough lips pressed once more against his own. And the whole world shivered with his solitude."

"That's it?" the stranger coughs, and coughs again.

"No," I say. "But it's late. I'll finish later. Good night." And I leave him there on my porch, bent like a clothespin, wheezing into the space between his knees.

He rests.

Hours passed before the stranger stirred. When at last he opened his eyes, the rain had stopped and the clouds had gone away. He pushed himself up on his side. He tried to spit, but something clogged his mouth. The sun lazed low in the sky, bathing half the world in pink while the other half reclined in shadow. The mud shone like barroom neon. Plastic bags rustled in the breeze. A hummingbird twitched from bush to bush. Birds sang to one another about topics of concern to birds. A few feet from the stranger's head, a spider dangled from a strand of silk, weaving itself a home among the weeds, its web shimmering a day-glo shade of orange. A beetle scaled a stalk of grass, while beneath it one thousand ants marched off in single file. Life delighted in life, but the stranger could not see it. He coughed up a clot of black blood and had no choice but to swallow it back down. He closed his eyes again.

When he woke, the sun was gone. It had not been replaced by the moon. The sky was black and blue and sometimes purple and if you looked at it hard enough it would turn other colors too. The stars — how can I begin to tell you about the stars? How many hairs are on your head, on your arms and on your legs? Count them if you can. How many have you already shed in the course of your life and how many more will you yet sprout? Count the ones in your ears, in your nostrils, on your toes and the backs of your arms. Count the ones between your legs as well. There were more stars still in the sky above the stranger, each one otherwise incomparable to hair, burning and bedazzling, as if the dark of night were the bagman's holey blanket stretched across the sky to hide a single flame, and each star just a pinpricked fragment of that blaze, with every wink and flicker begging the question: Why all this hiding? Why night at all? Why this filth and darkness? Why not just light and flame?

The stranger tried to rise, but lacked the strength, and fell back into the cold and sticky mud.

THREE

He is rescued.

Fine lines forked from the woman's eyes, and dug across her brow, but the eyes themselves were wide, and green, and youthful still. She dampened a cloth in a dented saucepan, and wiped the dirt and blood from the stranger's beard. His suit was a suit no more, so torn and begrimed that it could not even generously be termed a rag. She peeled it from his body and threw it in the fire. She washed him from callused sole to matted crown, and the water in her improvised washbasin went brown five times with the muck she wiped from his flesh, and five times she dumped the pan out empty in the bushes, refilled it at the drainage pipe, and again heated the water to a boil over the flames.

He endured this cleansing without complaint. He muttered something now and again, and if you had been there to hear him or if the woman who rescued him had been able to hear at all, you and she would have heard the words "now," "hereafter," and "I," as well as many words you and she had never heard before, and many sounds that might have been words or cries or just harrumphs, you and she would never know.

Every few hours his eyes opened wide and frenzied and

135

the woman jumped back in fright. Once his hand leapt forth and grabbed her by the wrist, the flesh of her arm at the same time plump and saggy. He pulled her close, but then his grip weakened and his eyes blinked shut as stupor washed over him again. The bruise on her wrist showed for days. Still, when the sweats came on, she wiped his brow with a moistened cloth, and when the shivers followed she swaddled him with blankets, with balled-up sweatshirts and unmatched woolen stockings, with everything she had. She covered his body with her own, as if hoping thereby not only to warm him but to absorb his convulsions, to pull them into her.

On the second day he woke long enough to drink some water, and when later, unconscious again, urine trickled down his thigh, she rolled him over and changed his bedding — piled strata of cast-off clothes laid in a roughly human shape on the dirt floor of her small shack. She left him for a while and came back with her pockets full. She brought a yellow onion, a wedge of cabbage, four limp stalks of celery and most of a baked potato, smeared with sour cream and crumbled bacon and wrapped in crumpled foil. She boiled it all into soup and when his eyelids next clicked open, she shoved a spoon between his lips. He spat the soup out, splattering her face. He jerked the spoon from her hand and hurled it off against the wall. Then his eyes clouded, and he rolled onto his side and slept.

On the third day, the stranger sat up. He tossed the blankets from his chest. She sat across the shack from him, her elbows on her knees, her heavy cheeks squeezed between her palms. The single room was illuminated by a burning wick in a half-filled bowl of kerosene. He gazed around at the leaning walls, one of green, corrugated fiberglass, one of sheet metal, two of warping particleboard. He stared into the lens of the scavenged camera that she had mounted on the wall above his head. No wire connected it to anything. The device watched and recorded nothing, but it made her feel less alone. He looked at her sitting on the floor before him, at the four skirts she wore one atop the other, the layered shirts on top. She wore three pairs of socks and two of stockings, but no shoes. He stared down at his own bare chest.

"Where is my suit?" the stranger said.

The woman did not answer. "My suit?" he asked again.

She shook her head, placed one finger on her lips and another on her ear, and shook her head once more.

The stranger nodded. "Dumb," he said. "You're dumb."

He ran his fingers over his chest and arms to indicate the absent garment, but the woman showed no sign of understanding. She stood, and retrieved from the surface of a small and wobbly table the bowl of soup, and the recovered spoon. She knelt beside him.

"No," he said, and waved her off. "Just go away."

That night she slept beside him, her fingers resting between the furrows of his ribs.

In the dirt.

The three of them kneeled around it in the dirt. "Looky looky," said the tall and skinny, pawing gently at the thing. The short and fat slapped his hand away. He cleared his throat. "Humbly, I take it upon myself to do the honors," he said, and tugged at the end of the string that bound what had until recently been the stranger's most treasured possession, the material form of his most desperate hopes.

"Hold on now," said the tall and fat. With meaty fingers, he grabbed the short and fat's wrist. "It's not your turn."

The short and fat stared at the hand that gripped his tattooed arm with exaggerated amazement, then shifted his gaze to his comrade's squinting eyes. "What's that there?" he asked "On my wrist? Squeezing me like that? Some kind of octopus, I think. A filthy squid. And us so far from the sea. I can't imagine how it got here."

The tall and skinny giggled. "Squid," he said.

"It's my turn," the tall and fat repeated, tightening his grip.

"It seems to be attached to your arm," the short and fat went on. "I can help you with that." With his left hand he pulled the straight razor from a back pocket of his jeans. He flicked it open. "Just hold still."

The tall and fat grinned wide. "My brother," he cooed. "You will eat that razor. I will carve Xs in your eyes."

"Maybe not so wise," the tall and skinny nodded in solemn agreement.

The short and fat let go of the string that wrapped the package and he and the tall and fat both slowly stood. The tall and fat's fat fingers still encircled the short and fat's fat arm. The razor glinted in the lamplight. Their eyes locked. They stepped in slow circles, dancing stiffly, motionless from the waist up. The package remained on the ground between them so that they resembled terrible, misshapen moons orbiting the same dull sun. A single eager, half-demonic grin contorted both their faces. They whispered words of love.

"Come on then," said the short and fat. "Come closer."

"Touch me," said the tall and fat. "Just once."

The tall and skinny crouched and waited as they turned until the moment came that neither of his comrades stood between him and the package. The tall and skinny took his opportunity. He scooped up the package, hooted, and wheeled about on his heel. But before he could lope away, the tall and fat and short and fat were on him. The tall and fat dove and swept his legs out with one huge extended arm. The short and fat hit him like a cannonball. The tall and skinny clattered to the ground. He lay there like a broken spider, his long limbs splayed at curious and unnatural angles. The tall and fat jumped on his back and yanked his arm up between his shoulder blades. The short and fat grabbed him by one earlobe, tugged his head up and held the razor to his throat.

"You've forgotten," he said into the tall and skinny's stretched, translucent ear. "You're not the smart one."

Just then the wind picked up. Something rustled across the dirt in front of them. All three looked up at once. It was the package. It had flown from the arms of the tall and skinny and landed a few yards off. It had come untied. The string lay flaccid on the ground. The oil-stained brown paper blew crumpled through the grass. It was empty. The three men leaped to their feet. They scoured the earth around them. They couldn't believe it. They looked everywhere, but all they found was rocks and dirt, broken bottle glass, fine, gray ash and sand.

I open the door.

When I open the door to my office, the stranger's sitting there. He's at my desk, in my chair. His suit is gone. He's wearing just a blanket. He doesn't look much better, but he's dry and most of the blood is gone. My papers, which I had left in neat stacks on my desk, have been scattered all around the room. They're crinkled and torn, as if a parade had just passed through. The stranger leans and retrieves a sheet from off the floor. He reads aloud, his voice striving for ridicule but too weak to pull it off. "Why all this hiding?" he scoffs. "Why night at all? Why this filth and darkness?" His fingers tremble as he tears the page in half. He pulls another page from the mess at his feet and reads, "It's okay baby wake up baby it's okay."

I take the page from his hand, smooth its creases with my thumb. "How long have you been here?" I ask.

"Long enough," he says.

"You do know, don't you, that I can always print another copy?"

He swivels around to face me. "I want to see the end."

"I haven't written it."

"Tell it to me."

I take off my jacket, hang it on the hook on the back of the door. "Get off my chair," I say.

To my surprise, he does. With a modesty that is almost touching, he gathers the blanket around him, stiffly stands. His legs are pale and hairless and marbled with welts. He looks like a cartoon stork. Papers crumple beneath him as he lowers himself, hunching, onto the couch. "Do you want to hear the rest of the story?" I say.

"The little boy?" he sniffs.

"Yeah, the little boy."

"That's not the story I was talking about."

"I'm afraid you don't have a choice," I say. I begin where I left off:

"When at last the little boy roused himself again, he did not feel hope, but anger. He took no joy this time from the warmth of the sun, finding in it only a dim, more distant likeness of the rage that burned within him. How dare the little girl desert him? How dare the bird, the fish, the rabbit, the dog, all the creatures he had kissed to life?

"He gathered thorns, nails, tacks, rusted and serrated blades, razor wire, hard and pointed stones, ground glass, barrels of bubbling industrial waste. With these he built a shark. He spat upon its head and sent it off to chase the fish. He built a hawk to fall upon the rabbit. He cursed it to life and with a flutter of feathers hurled it in the air. He built a snake, filled its teeth with poison, and kicked it down the path where the little girl might skip and the dog might curl itself to sleep. Just in case, he built a man and a woman. He slapped and spat them awake, bid them wreck whatever the others chanced to miss. He built a vulture so as not to leave a mess.

"Exhausted by his efforts, the little boy laid down beneath a tree to rest. But his heart would not slow. Even when he closed his eyes, he saw the branches above him thrashing in rhythm with his pulse. In fact the tree was still. The wind sang softly through the grass, but all the little boy could hear was shrieking, gnashing, tearing. He picked at the grass, twisted it into rope, tore the rope, twisted the tearings into a cord again. Repeat.

"Sleep fled before him as everything else had. Wakefulness had lost what little charm it held. He shook the leaves from his clothes. If he could find only displeasure here, perhaps elsewhere he might find rest. Or something like it. Some variety of relief. Perhaps, it occurred to him, as he let his feet fall one after the other, he had not given his creations a chance. Perhaps they had been playing. Perhaps they had run, intending that he give chase. Perhaps they were wondering where he was, feeling as injured by his absence as he was by theirs. Perhaps. Insomnia weakens the workings of the mind. But it allowed the little boy to indulge in a species of optimism that gave purpose to his wanderings. Perhaps, he consoled himself, he would find what he had lost, and be welcomed by it."

The stranger's eyes have closed. He lets himself fall slowly onto his side and rests his head on the arm of the couch. He pulls his blanket up to his beard. My papers, these pages, lie crumpled all around him.

"I'll finish later," I say.

He speaks without opening his eyes. "Are you trying," he asks, "to tell me something?"

He journeys out.

The stranger tried to walk. His rescuer stood beside him, one hand on his elbow, the other around his back. "Don't. Touch. Me," he hissed. But she could not hear him, and after three steps, he let himself lean into her and limped onward with her support, adding another hissed *don't-touch-me* as he did.

He made it out the door and a few feet outside the shack before he stumbled. His legs were not the problem. His ribs were broken, his organs bruised; he grew weaker with each step. The woman caught him and lowered him in her arms to the ground. The stranger lay there naked on the dirt, and before she could bend to drag him back inside to bed, he was able to crane his head around and see where he had landed.

The deaf-mute's shack sat on a small plateau of level earth midway up the slope between the railroad tracks below and a concrete embankment just up the hill. A cement overpass provided shelter from the elements, and the woman's dwelling was protected on all sides by tangled shrubbery — the skeletal remains of oleanders long-since cannibalized by kudzu. A wan poinsettia protruded from a flowerpot beside the door. Dried and wilted flowers lay in heaps. Rank upon rank of plastic baby dolls guarded the hovel — some pink, some brown, most nude but some dressed in soiled jumpers, some with hair and some without, others without heads but still standing on alert, their feet planted in the soil. Behind this plastic phalanx, other goods lay piled: blenders and toasters, a vacuum cleaner and two broken-screened TVs, the backseat from a Ford, a plush giraffe, more flowerpots, all empty, a sombrero'd Mexican lawn jockey with a cracked ceramic beer mug foaming in his hand. Off to the right a drainage pipe projected from the hillside, and from its lip water dribbled forth. An iron grill sat atop a circle of blackened bricks and concrete blocks a few feet in front of the car seat, still smoking from the night before.

"Quite a grand estate you have," the stranger began to say. Before he could finish the phrase, though, as if in response, the dolls all turned to face him. Or seemed to turn, it's hard to say — the stranger wasn't feeling well. The dolls stood at attention, straightening what spines they had (none really) and clicking together their fat, naked heels, though the effect, since they were plastic, was more soft thud than click. Each kicked out a right leg, then a left. They goose-stepped solemnly in place. Pudgy ankles rising, falling, here and there catching glints of sun. Those that had heads held their heads high. Each doll reached to the doll beside it. They partnered off, clasping one hand straight out in front and placing the other in the very small small of their partners' plastic backs. They tangoed as elegantly as broken and discarded dolls can tango, filing off pair by pair and dancing, arms extended, in straight lines towards the stranger, stopping just out of his reach, twirling their hips, switching hands and dancing back. When all had had a chance, the dolls decoupled. Stiff-legged, they marched in place, showing him the soles of their varyingly booted and unbooted feet. The stranger groaned. The dolls all curtsied. The woman, smiling, lifted the stranger from beneath the arms to pull him back inside. Did she see what the stranger saw? Did dead things come alive for him alone? To salute him or to mock him? Was it the deaf-mute's doing? Did anyone see it but he and you and I? It's hard to say. The stranger's eyes were shut. He bit his lip, and let himself be pulled.

Searching.

Searching, they found nothing but searchers. They walked all day every day. They asked all those they came across if they had seen the man in the ragged white suit. Usually the old man asked because words came to him most easily. Too easily, sometimes, and with too many other words attached. "You haven't seen him, huh? Too bad. Maybe not for you, though, right? Maybe okay for you. Cause really, who's fool enough to want to encounter such an individual, besides my companions here, and my sorry old self?"

They met two crippled twins outside a bowling alley who shook their heads in unison and wheeled along beside them. The twins required no convincing, no long explanations. They seemed to know what the men were looking for before they even asked. Or maybe not. Perhaps they were looking for something completely different, a buried treasure, misplaced keys or a kidnapped terrier, and their path happened to coincide precisely with that of the bagman, the old man and the preacher. No matter, they were searching too.

They met a long-haired teenage girl carrying a yellow-nozzled red plastic gas can. It was empty. Her car had run out of fuel, and when the old man asked her to join them, she thought for a while, then shrugged and asked, "Why not?" No one had an answer for her, and she did not expect one, so none was good enough. They met an old prostitute in tennis shoes with a black eye and sagging knees. She had never seen no one never, she insisted, but then she tagged along a quarter block behind them. They met a small gang of boys in baseball caps and windbreakers who would not any of them answer the old man's queries, who just stood and gaped at them with fear and revulsion in their eyes.

They slept in alleys and beneath the hedges that limned the parking lots of malls. They took turns bathing in gas station restrooms. "A bird bath for a funny, funny bird," the old man said, shaking the water from his hands and winking at the long-haired girl. "A funny flock of birds." They ate at minimarts and at liquor stores where bulletproof dividers separated the merchants from their wares. The preacher bought individually wrapped donuts and styrofoam cups of instant soup, but never shared his meals. The bagman endured stern glares from the preacher for shoplifting frozen burritos. He thawed them beneath his sweater and gave everyone a piece. The old man always refused his share. He didn't seem to eat anything at all.

No one had seen the white-suited stranger, or would admit to having seen him. Deprived entirely of clues, his seekers had no reason to choose one direction over another, so they marched in concentric circles, in an unfolding spiral, to cover as much surface area as possible without having to commit to any single — and perhaps mistaken — bearing. Freeways got in their way, and gated lots, so they zigzagged where they had to. They spent two days following a man with an eye patch who told them he had received a coded message from the stranger on his transistor radio and knew precisely where he was, but who, when pressed for details would only sweep his arm broadly and shout, "Right over here, I'm telling you, right here." A fat woman in a pink sweatsuit fell in with them. A cockatiel perched on her shoulder. "Think you're much?" the bird screeched every twelve minutes, morning and night, "Know you're living?" The long-haired girl threatened to strangle it, and the fat woman called her a skank. A three-legged greyhound trailed limping behind them, all ribs and half bald. The old man began lifting shrink-wrapped sandwiches and pre-sliced poundcake to feed it. Twice a police car shadowed them, cruising slowly behind them until without incident they crossed an invisible line dividing the municipality from the one that flanked it, at which point their pursuers lost interest in the chase.

Mainly they were silent. The preacher's sandwich board beat against his calves. The lenses strung around his neck rattled against the board and against one another. The bagman's bags rustled on his back. The wheels of the cripples' wheelchairs squeaked, and the two of them conversed in rare whispers in a language known only to one another. The bird squawked right on schedule. Their feet collected calluses and blisters and the soles of their shoes wore thinner as they plodded down the pavement, across the avenues, and through the broken fields.

Sometimes the old man whistled, and sometimes he talked. The preacher scowled when he approached. He took this as encouragement and, with a spark of mischief in his eye, started in. "I don't want you to take this wrong," the old man began, "but have you ever considered another profession? I mean, something more suited to your strengths?" But the preacher could walk faster than the old man, and soon outdistanced him without a word in response.

Flushing the urinal in a QuickMart men's room, the old man chatted up the twins as they sat wheel to wheel, brushing their teeth before the sink. He pointed to the video camera mounted on the tiled wall above the mirror. "You ever wonder," the old man said, "if anybody's watching?" The twins exchanged panicked glances. They looked at each other, at the camera, at the old man's reflection in the mirror. Someone had scratched the words "Sureños rifan putos" in the glass. "I don't just mean the cameras," the old man continued. "Cause who could have time to watch all those things? It's hard enough to keep an eye on what's right in front of you. I'm talking about inside, inside your head. I mean who's watching there? Who's keeping track? Like when you say you don't know how you feel about something and you decide to listen to your thoughts, to keep an eye on yourself, who's doing the listening? Who's watching and who's being watched?" In unison, the twins shook their heads and spat toothpaste into the sink. "Everything keeps splitting in two," the old man said. "Know what I mean?" As they wheeled out of the room without a word, the old man grinned. "Course you do," he said.

He tried to tell the man with the eye patch a story about his wife. "She was not a small woman," he began, "and I don't mean that she was fat, though she wasn't svelte. She was what they call big-boned, and tall to boot. First time I kissed her I made sure we were standing on a flight of stairs, and that she was three steps below me. Her tongue was the size of my whole face. I fell for her right there and then. I could climb her legs like trees. She'd cradle me like an infant in her arms. That's the kind of girl for me, you lay her down, you need a sextant and a clear sky to navigate your way across."

The man with the eye patch hid his ear behind his radio and broke into a jog. The old man tried again to chat up the cripples but they just nodded and said things he didn't understand. The prostitute avoided him. The cockatiel talked, but it didn't seem to listen and it always said the same thing. Its owner was no better a conversationalist. "Oh no," she'd say whenever she saw him coming, "don't you get me started."

The old man winked at the long-haired girl and asked her why she'd joined them. "You're a pretty girl," he said, "what're you running with these fools for?" She dug in her pack for a cigarette, but didn't answer. "Oh," said the old man, raising his eyebrows. "I see how it is. Someone went and broke your heart."

The girl's shoulders dropped a little. Her eyes fell to her feet, and the old man knew that he was right. His old man's heart felt heavy, and he wanted to tell her not to take it too hard, not to hold on to it too long or too tight. He wanted to warn her to get used to it, that love is not the substance of this world. Maybe of some other one. Here the planets spin on yearning. But instead he laid a hand on her shoulder and said, "Don't worry kid. There's lots of fellas out there." She shook him off and rushed ahead, hugging the empty gas can.

They walked all day, over steep, treeless hills, through weedy, smog-choked valleys. They followed the train tracks until a security guard chased them back into the streets. When at last they stopped to rest in the shade of an awning behind an empty warehouse, the old man crouched beside the bagman. The bagman pulled a piece of peanut brittle from a pocket, dusted off the lint, and offered it to the old man. The old man smiled gratefully, but shook his head. "You really seen him, huh?" he asked.

The bagman nodded, and took a bite.

"And you just knew it was him?"

The bagman nodded again.

"What was he like?" the old man asked.

The bagman considered the question carefully and took his time in answering. "Tall," he said at last.

"I suppose he would be. He kind of acts more like a short guy though."

"He wasn't short," the bagman said. After a long while he spoke again. "He slept real bad."

The old man grinned. "As well he should." He shifted his weight from one knee to the other. "What do you think will happen," he asked the bagman, "when you find him?"

The bagman looked around as if expecting to find the words he needed waiting on a tree branch or perched on the eaves of the warehouse roof. He couldn't find them.

"You can't help him," the old man said. "You know that, don't you?"

"He's carrying too much stuff," the bagman answered.

The old man gestured at the bagman's bags. "And you think you're the one to help him with that?"

The bagman's eyes scoured the pavement in front of him as if he might find an answer for the old man there. He scratched himself, and squinched his face, and when he finally opened his mouth to answer, the cockatiel cut him off.

"Think you're much?" it screeched, "Know you're living?"

The old man laughed, and the bagman almost smiled.

He performs a miracle.

In the evening, the stranger lay on his back and watched the
shadows chase one another about the walls as a breeze shook the
wick of the lamp. The woman kneeled at his feet and watched
him watch. His eyes turned to her, to the lamplight dancing
across the rounded contours of her face. What she saw frightened her profoundly. It wasn't hatred, and it would be hard to
call it cruel. It was a hunger that had nothing to do with her, to
which her presence was so completely incidental that she felt
herself in danger.

"Come here," he said to her, and motioned her forward
with one crooked finger. She pointed doubtfully to her breast,
as if perhaps he were mistaken. The stranger nodded. "Yes, you."

The woman's back was hunched with fear as she crawled
on her knees to the stranger's side. He sat up, and gestured for
her to lean closer to his face. "Here," he said. "Come here." She
closed her eyes, and leaned in towards him. She was shaking.
The stranger took the deaf woman's head between his hands and
cupped his palms over her ears. "Hear," he said. "Hear me." He
ran his fingertips down along her jaws and stuck the thumb and
forefinger of each hand between her lips and into her mouth.
She squirmed as he grabbed her tongue.

"Speak," he said, yanking her tongue out past her teeth.
"Hear me and speak."

With his palm on her brow, the stranger pushed the woman from him. She fell back, and when she opened her eyes she
regarded him at first with puzzlement. He had not hurt her.
Then a grin crept across her face. With her mouth clamped

shut to hide her broken teeth, she reached forward and cupped her own small palms over his ears. She waited a moment to see what he would do and, when he did nothing, she ran her fingers down through his white sideburns and beard. She stroked at his lips with the pads of her thumbs. They were cracked, his lips were, and bleeding still. She pulled them back and down so that he looked like a child making monkey faces. Devoid entirely of mockery, her grin stretched until it could grow no wider, then took living form as laughter, the first sound she had produced since the stranger's arrival, a sort of low and choking glee.

The stranger swatted her hands from his face and, with what little strength remained to him, he shoved the woman away. She skidded across the small, dark room. Her hair covered her face until she sat up, shook it off, and leaned her back against the quivering fiberglass wall, gagging and burbling and laughing still.

"Idiot," the stranger barked.

The long night.

Pigeon told his sisters nothing. They had begun to bug him, demanding that he tell them where he ran off to each morning. His older sister had noticed, though she did not mention this to Pigeon, that certain things about him had changed in the space of just two days. He did not kick every rock he came across, for instance, and he no longer circled every tree. He bobbed along undistracted in a more or less straight line. Maybe he had a girlfriend, the older sister speculated to the younger. The younger cackled and jumped at the hilarity of the thought: Pigeon kissing a girl. She stuck out her tongue and made her eyes go googly. Really though, it wasn't girls that worried Pigeon's older sister. Girls she could take care of. It was adults that worried her, and boys that liked to hurt things.

On the third day after his discovery, he managed to lose them both. The older girl woke up before he did, but he dashed off while she was peeing and the little one was too slow to catch him. He took as circuitous a route as he could, stomping down the grass on false paths and doubling back in case they tried to follow. He spent the whole day bouncing, lost in the rhythm of it: the almost weightless sense of expectation as his feet left the trampoline; the feeling, as he flew upwards, that he might never stop, that he might this time break free forever of gravity's hold and henceforth cruise weightless through the clouds; and then the brief but crushing disappointment as he lost momentum, seemed to stop a moment in midair, and fell again to start the cycle over. How could he share this bliss?

That night Pigeon dreamed of the trampoline. He was

with his mother and his sisters. The four of them held hands and bounced in a circle together, singing as they rose and fell a song so beautiful that it made his eyes hurt. In the morning, when he woke, his sister was already up. She saw his eyes blink open and immediately pounced. She sat on his chest. "You're not going anywhere without me," she said.

Pigeon yawned and tried to shove her off. "Okay," he said. "Get off me."

He didn't tell them what it was. He led them through the bushes and the brambles, down the dirt road and under the bridge, through the yards and down the alley. As they got closer, pride quickened Pigeon's steps. To his surprise, he felt no irritation at his sisters' presence. For the moment at least, his heart thrilled at the thought of seeing joy bounce in their eyes.

He led them across the lot and around the final corner. There it was, the heaped expanse of bricks. And in the middle: Nothing. Just more bricks. The trampoline was gone. Pigeon stood silent. His lower lip protruding. The bricks dug into his soles. "It was here," he said.

Hip cocked, his older sister tapped her foot. "What was here?" she asked.

How could something so big just disappear?

Pigeon tried to explain, but he could not. The portal had closed. It would not reopen here. His sisters did not believe him. They suspected him of untold disloyalties and crimes. He was not sure that they were wrong. Why else would he be punished?

For the next few days, he avoided them. He slipped out extra early, and wandered with no goal in mind except to search for what he'd lost, and if not to actually find it, to somehow shake off his shame and disbelief. He bobbed through the lots and the alleys, counting his steps, kicking logs and circling rocks, knocking on everything, three times, five times, sometimes up to seven. Odd numbers that could not be divided.

One night Pigeon did not go home. Sunset found him lost, and far from the makeshift shelter in which the three of them had lately slept. The darkness gathered. A dog barked and a minute later barked again. The second bark sounded closer than the first, so Pigeon climbed a tree and squatted in the crotch of its three conjoining trunks. The tree's rough flesh scratched his ankles and his arms. He tried to sleep, but it was cold without his sisters there to hold him, and he was frightened by the sounds the night made. Somewhere the dog kept barking, sometimes close and sometimes far. An owl hooted. He could not see it, but he could hear the air whoosh through its wings as it swept low beneath the branches. Far off he thought he heard music sometimes, men shouting, breaking glass. Frogs croaked as if they were much larger beasts. Pigeon drifted off, but the moment his muscles eased towards slumber, he woke, fearing he would fall. Shapes appeared and disappeared, bringing noises with them. Shadows swelled and shriveled. The leaves trembled with the breeze. Pigeon thought of his two sisters, the warmth of their small bodies, the smell of them.

At last the sky began to lighten. If only because the night was over, Pigeon was thankful for the day. He climbed down, his limbs stiff from shivering. He circled the tree three times and knocked seven times on each of its three trunks to be sure he hadn't missed something. His head hurt from hunger and his legs felt weak. He walked to the next tree and the next, circling each one and rapping on its trunk, varying slightly his pattern of knocks, then re-testing previously abandoned patterns, inspecting each tree's bark and tugging at its lowest branches. In this manner Pigeon found his way out of the woods and into a clearing of trampled dirt beside which stretched the railroad tracks. He was relieved: he could find his way home eventually, he knew, by following the tracks. For a moment his chin stopped bobbing. He kicked at a crumpled ball of oil-stained brown paper, but it was too heavy with dew to roll very far.

On the ground he spied a soiled length of twine. He grabbed one end and pulled it, but it was attached to nothing and came up limp in his hand. He dropped the string, and noticed beside it a curious stone. It was not gray or brown or white like the other stones around it. It appeared to simultaneously contain all colors and to be no color at all, to shine and to be dull. Pigeon picked it up and saw that it was not a stone, but a shard of bone. It felt warm in his hand but made his flesh feel cold. He held it to his eye and saw that he'd been wrong. It was not a shard of bone. It was a diamond, tarnished with dust and as big as the top joint of his thumb. He took a breath, closed his fingers over it, and looked around to be sure no one had seen him. When he opened them again his hand concealed no precious gem, just the tiny, cold, wet body of a mouse. He jumped and dropped the thing. But kneeling to look at it, he found no mouse there, no diamond, bone or rock, just a slender dagger, its haft hammered from the same dark steel as its blade. It fit perfectly in Pigeon's palm and when he held it all the anguish of his long night seemed to spread up his arm and to fill his ribs to bursting. He felt chilled from the inside out. The agony of his smallness, his aloneness, his inability to protect or be protected seemed to course like a current through his bones. It hurt him terribly. The dagger lengthened. Pigeon's chin shivered and tears rolled down his cheeks. He could not let go of it. He held the thing as far from his body as he could. The trees in front of him glowed a gentle orange. They quivered for a moment and appeared to bleed before bursting softly into flame.

He journeys out, again.

When the sun's first light slithered through the hovel's doorway, the stranger was already standing. The woman slept on the floor at his feet. Her hair hung over her mouth, and rose and fell with her every intake of breath. The stranger wrapped a blanket around his waist. He kicked the woman awake. "Come on," he said. He grabbed her by the shoulder and growled, "don't touch me," but she of course did not hear him, and smiled at his touch. She squeezed his hand, rubbed the sleep from her eyes and followed as he, lips white and spine unyielding, staggered on outdoors.

This time all the dolls but one ignored him. A red-headed doll with a pink, stockinged face turned away from him and bent at the waist, showing the stranger its cleft, molded buttocks and winking up through its legs. The others stood inanimate, staring dumb and dead through long-lashed eyes as the stranger and the deaf-mute hurried by.

On the other side of the bulwark of brush, the world opened up to them. Everything was a sharp yellowish-pink, not yet drained of color by the day. Sirens wailed somewhere off to their right. In the opposite direction, the one from which the stranger had arrived some days before, thick woods rose all around the train tracks. Directly beneath him, though, a wide lot had been cleared of trees, and was still swampy from the rain. A heron stood there with one foot in the murk, waiting, apparently, for fish. To its right, the rear ends of warehouses and factories flanked the tracks, and from the slight height at which he and the deaf-mute woman stood, the stranger could see suburbs stretching off into the distance: an endless and unvaried plain of box-like structures with flat tarpaper roofs, the uniformity of the terrain broken only by the occasional wide boulevard and by outcroppings of billboards and high plastic signs, some of them slowly rotating, boasting of gasoline, donuts, hamburgers, liquor, live nude girls, quik and e-z oil changes. Smoke, almost scarlet in the morning light, obscured the horizon. Many of the buildings appeared to be on fire.

He stumbled down the slope, falling twice, not looking at the woman as she labored to help him up. They walked along the tracks toward the town, stepping with care from one tie to the next. Every ten or twelve steps, the stranger would pause, lean against the woman, and catch his breath. After a few minutes of slow and jerky progress, he lurched away and pulled her down to recline on the ballast and rest. The stranger was sitting there in his blanket, clutching his ribs, the deaf-mute woman beside him, reaching out with one tentative hand to stroke his hair, when three boys came running down the tracks. Two were thin and one was fat. The stranger had encountered them before. They wore torn windbreakers. Their faces were blackened from smoke. One wore a backwards baseball cap. They passed within a yard of the woman and the stranger. The panicked eyes of the first two took in nothing but the ground in front of them, and hardly that, and they ran on without pause. The last one though, the fat one, saw the stranger there and froze. He looked at the stranger and then at his own feet before noticing that his friends had run off without him, that he was alone. With a grunted "wait up," he sprinted on to join them.

The stranger laughed at the apparition. "Where's your friend?" he yelled after the boys, and to himself chuckled,

"There were four," but his fractured ribs had not yet healed, and laughter hurt him, so he clutched his chest in pain. Using the woman's head for support, he pushed himself to his feet again.

They walked and paused and walked and rested, and as the smell of smoke grew sharper, the stranger's grip on the woman's shoulder grew tighter, and her steps became more hesitant. The sirens stopped. No birds sang. Ash lingered in the air like snowflakes on a windless day. At last they passed beneath a trestle and over a bridge, and reached the outmost ring of fire. The warehouses on both sides of the tracks were burning. The flames were blue, and green, and looked more like water than fire, a light, defiant liquid, able to skip, and leap, and burn. The earth on all sides of them had turned a glistening black. It bubbled and oozed and hardened fast in jagged, glassy peaks. The warehouses crumbled soundlessly. The flames faded. The earth hissed.

As if quickened and strengthened by the heat, the stranger scampered suddenly off the tracks and up through the ash to the top of the embankment. The woman ran beside him. He stopped at the top and gazed off into the fires, as if searching for someone or for something. For blocks, the sidewalks boiled. Shop windows danced and shimmered like the surface of a storm-tossed sea. Angels of smoke advanced in ordered legions across the sky, blowing banks of ash before them. The stranger's eyes focused on the point of calm, perhaps a mile off, from which the conflagrations seemed to radiate. But it was too far, even for eyes as sharp as his, to make out the crumpled silhouette of Pigeon crying.

The stranger's strength deserted him. His features paled, then darkened. "Let's go," he said, and turned around. After seven steps, his knees gave out, so the woman laid him in the blanket, and dragged him home.

I finish my story.

The helicopter wakes me again. Not the searchlight this time, just the din of it, that low, thwacking drone growing louder then low then loud again as the helicopter orbits above. It wakes her too beside me, but just long enough to blink once or twice, groan, and roll over into sleep. I lie on my back and watch the ceiling fan spin and the camera light flicker as it's obscured by the blade on each rotation. Her hair spreads across the pillow, tickles my chin. Her fist clenches and unclenches on my chest. Somewhere I hear the faint yowl of a siren and then another one, closer than the first, rouses the neighborhood dogs and gives pause to the coyotes, who are already awake, padding through the streets and the alleys. All of them join in, the dogs locked each in their backyard pens, the coyotes at large in the shadows, all of them together howling with the ambulance and the cop car or the fire truck, becoming for just a moment a single, unbroken, primal pack, united by one inchoate thirst that stretches up from yard to yard and street to street across the city.

I get up, slip on my slippers, find a clean-ish t-shirt on the floor. In the kitchen, I pour myself a finger of whisky, and then another finger. I sit on the couch, feel between the cushions for the remote and with it click the television on. The TV takes a moment to blink to life but when it does the image is strange, a blurred, quivering, greenish black and white. It looks like someone being filmed from above, sitting hunched on a sofa, sipping at a drink. I get up to check the cables and the someone on the screen gets up too. It's me. He is. I look up and to the right at the camera bolted to the ceiling. The guy on the screen does too.

I can see him out of the corner of my eye. He looks out, through the lens, right at me. Looped again. Fucking camera interfering with the reception. I slap the TV and the image shifts. Another blurred and static shot, this one blinking twice a second from green to black and back again. A bed, also shot from above. A furrowed landscape of bunched up sheets. A bare arm hanging off the bed. A fan blade obscures the lens, circles back, again. The camera in the bedroom. I turn the television off.

I empty my drink, pour myself another and bring the glass outside with me to the porch. The siren's gone and the dogs have gone to sleep again. The stars are dim. The moon, tentative, half full, hovers just above the horizon. The crickets shriek. The power lines sway in the breeze. A streetlight flickers, and in its yellow light I see a shape on the concrete path just beneath the steps to the porch. It's a body. I reach inside, turn on the porch-light. I half expect to find a drunk, or someone overdosed or stabbed, but it's the stranger. Face down. He wears no clothes. I can see his long white hair, his dull scapula jutting like wings, his bare and skinny buttocks.

I go inside and pull a sheet from the closet. I can't say why, but I don't want to touch his naked skin. Or I don't want it to touch me. I roll him onto the sheet, lift him up and bring him in. He's as light as a child, brittle and gangly, as if no tendons connect his bones. I can feel the heat of him through the sheet and even in the dark of the living room I can see the fever sweat beading on his temples and brow. His hair is damp with it. He doesn't wake.

I lay him out on the couch and wipe the sweat from his forehead with a corner of the sheet. His breath rattles slow and uneven through his nose. I sip my drink. I stroke his beard, rest my palm on his brow. "Listen," I begin, though I know he cannot hear me, "The little boy found everything. He found the dog. It had eaten the rabbit and been stung by the snake. It looked as it had before he'd kissed it: a greasy towel hung sloppily over wire hangers, broken pots. The hawk in turn had eaten the snake, but the man and the woman had toppled the tree in which it made its nest. It broke a wing. The vulture had taken care of the rest.

"The little boy swam. He scoured the sea for the fish and the shark, but he did not find them anywhere. Sitting on the shore, he noticed that the skin on his arms and his legs and his boyish belly had broken out in small but angry boils. His eyes stung. His lungs hurt when he breathed. He understood: the man and woman had poisoned the sea, as men and women do. Thus the absence of the fish and the shark, and of the man and the woman as well.

"The little boy heard the vulture laugh. He turned and saw it sitting in the low branch of a tall tree, just where the dunes gave way to swollen hills. And in a valley between two hills, immediately beneath the tree in which the vulture sat, the little boy found the little girl. Her arms and legs were bare and thin and speckled with bruises and the dotted lines of scrapes. In her hands she held the first of the little boy's creations, the bird. Climbing a tree — the same scabby tree in which the vulture now waited — she had found the bird's nest and grabbed it before it could fly away. She had clutched it to her chest and scaled the branches in reverse. And sitting there on the ground, just moments before the little boy arrived, curiosity had compelled the little girl to twist the bird's tiny head around, to see how far it would turn. It turned all the way around.

"She sat, puzzled by the stillness of the thing in her hand, the tiny wings that had so recently been atwitch with frustrated flight. 'It won't move,' she said to the boy.

"From the tree, the vulture laughed again. The little boy turned to look at it. It was much fatter than it had been when he'd built it.

"He looked back at the girl, who looked down at the bird. Tears washed clean lines through the dirt that smudged her cheeks. The little boy was not able to cry anymore, but standing there between the little girl and the vulture, he felt a grief deeper than any he had previously felt. Though he was only a boy, he was wise enough to understand that he himself was made of want, and that though he had tried to build something other than himself, something that might fill his absences, he had succeeded only at building more want, want chasing want chasing want, like the tears that raced down the girl's cheekbones to her chin. But love is also want.

"The little boy had nowhere else to go, so he sat beside the little girl. And there the four of them remained — the little boy, the little girl, the dead bird and the live one — until the sun's light dimmed and the sky's smaller lights switched on one by one. Some of the lights were the planets that the little boy had made. They swung in wide ellipses round his head. Others though, were faraway stars with orbits of their own, planets of their own, and even moons. The space between the stars belonged to no one, and as many stars as there were — as many moons and planets and belts of silent rocks — its bright blackness took up most of the sky. The little boy sat. The little girl sat. The vulture sat. The dead bird too. Above them swirled the sky. Some stars blinked out. Others exploded. Here and there, new stars shined."

I lift the stranger's sleeping head and slide a pillow beneath it. I spread a blanket over him. "That's the end," I say. "Good night."

He is consoled, again.

The stranger's fever returned. All day he muttered, cursed, and spat. He thrashed and kicked when the woman came too near. Sometimes he shook his index finger in the air, his fist squeezed tight, issuing decrees to the dim. What words did he pronounce? His throat was parched — she could not make him drink — and his tongue was thick with fever, but had you been there to hear, and brave enough to lean in close, you would have heard a lot of things, strange, self-serving apologies directed at the stars, justifications so thick with self-deceit that you'd need Q-tips doused with oven cleaner to cleanse your ears on hearing them. Once he sat up straight and the film covering his eyes seemed to clear for a moment. He laughed a high, phlegmy laugh and said, "So the doctor tells the priest, 'You're gonna be just fine, the only thing is you'll have to keep this bag attached to you at all times.'" But then all energy abandoned him. His eyes blinked closed and his spine went limp again. He slept for half a day, waking only to moan, roll his head and clack his jaws.

The woman sat beside him. Had she been able to come up with the words, she would have tried to comfort him with what little truth she felt she had a claim on. As a girl, she had seen the ocean once. She had sat in the back of her mother's boyfriend's car for hour after hour. She'd had to pee. She didn't remember which boyfriend it had been, but she remembered the ridged blue vinyl of the seats, sticky with sweat beneath her thighs, the metal buckle of the seat belt hot from the sun and burning the inside of her wrist, her bladder near bursting as treetops and clouds floated past outside. Then she looked out

the window and saw that the trees and the houses and billboards had all disappeared and there was nothing outside the
car but the huge and patient green and rolling sea. What was it
doing out there? She still saw it in her dreams, saw how it toyed
with the land and the air, and had she been able, she would have
told her guest about it. She would have told him that the sea
was deep and that the air rose up forever above it, but that the
line separating ocean from atmosphere is thinner than a line,
is always moving, always shifting, always changing. She would
have tried to tell him that the same is true for everything worth
anything, that below it all is dark and cold, and above it's just
endless yawning emptiness, and that that line which is not a
line is never ever still and never fixed but it is always there and
if it were not, water would not be water and air would not be
air. But she could not tell him this, or anything, and she knew
he would not listen if she could. Instead she mopped the sweat
from his brow whenever he would let her.

In the evening, he slept, and she lay at his side. When the
shakes took hold of him again, she again stretched her body on
top of his. She held his wrists. She placed her mouth over his,
and felt his breath on her lips and on her teeth. She kissed his
eyelids, and when his trembling at last stopped, she sucked the
stranger's tongue into her mouth. He did not stir. With her eye-
lashes she brushed at his nose and cheeks. She lifted the covers
and traced with her finger his jutting bones. The sharpness of
his hips. The hollows beneath them. She sucked at his lip and
licked the dry roof of his mouth. She lifted her many shirts until her heavy breasts fell forth. She lowered one to the strangers'
mouth, but he lay still. She tried the other one. With her fingers, she pried open his lips, and placed a nipple between them.

He lay inert, so she took his fingers in her mouth. She ran her breasts over his eyelids, then down along his throat and chest. She rubbed her nipples against his nipples, her groin against his groin. She felt him stirring there, so she stroked him with her palm, squatted over him and lifted up her many skirts. His eyes blinked open as she lowered herself on top of him. His jaw stiffened. "Don't touch," he groaned, but then his eyes rolled upwards and his head rolled back, and he tugged her down around him hard, his fists balled on her wide hips. His body jerked twice into hers. His face twisted as if overcome by sudden agony. Whatever force had briefly lent him animation drained out of him, suddenly and entirely. She licked the sweat from his chest. His eyelids fluttered when she kissed them. They slept.

Goodbyes.

They felt the smoke before they smelled it. A fit of coughing overtook the old man and he had to sit and, gasping, wait it out. The bagman helped him up. The cockatiel stopped talking. Then the light changed and they began to smell the burning in the air. They did not know what it was or who it was, but they all felt certain they were getting close to something. The preacher nervously fingered the trigger of his bullhorn and every few seconds a burble of static belched from its gray mouth.

A cloud of birds flew over them. Not just one species, but many intermixed. Gulls and crows and screaming jays. A great blue heron, its long neck folded, flapped its giant wings. Above it flew a finch. Doves flew next to swallows, sparrows beside hawks. Enough of them that for a space of several seconds the humans advancing beneath could feel the air chill as the shadows of the birds passed over. They all flew in the same direction, away from the smoke and the flames toward which the pilgrims walked, unknowing. The cockatiel squawked and snapped on its master's shoulder. It spread its yellow wings and, without a further damning word, launched itself into the air to join its kind in flight.

The woman in the pink sweatsuit fell to her knees, her mouth stuck open like an italic letter *O*. The old man helped her stand and put his arm around her, ignoring the milky strings of bird crap that had crusted on her shoulders. "Don't worry," he lied. "He'll be back."

But the woman did not believe him. She pushed away his

arm and spun suddenly around. Eyes on the smoke-clogged heavens, she ran after her pet.

After that, they saw no more birds. They saw no squirrels, no rats, no deer or feral dogs. Even the insects appeared to have evacuated. The pilgrims marched onward through the woods, the twins rearing to force their wheelchairs over roots and fallen tree limbs. They heard something crashing through the leaves. A skinny little boy ran towards them, his head bobbing furiously up and down. The boy's palms were blackened with soot. He held them out on thin brown arms stretched far in front of him as he ran, as if trying to push something away, to hurl it from his grasp. His face was wet with sweat or tears and though he was running, his eyes were squeezed shut. He was gone before they could stop him. They turned to watch Pigeon's little brown body disappear through the trees. The greyhound turned tail and scuttled after him.

They still could not see the fire, but when they began to feel its heat the man with the eye patch started to mutter to himself. The muttering steadily rose in volume and in pitch until the man was spitting curses. The preacher twirled around to face him and when he did the man with the eye patch backed away and stumbled, then brushed himself off and began walking hurriedly backwards in the direction from which they'd come. The twins exchanged quick glances and wheeled away behind him.

"I gotta go," said the long-haired girl to no one in particular.

"We're getting close," the old man told her with a wink.

She frowned. "To what?" she asked.

The old man laughed. "That is the question, isn't it?" But his laughter turned quickly to coughing and while he was bent there, his hands on his knees, the long-haired girl said one word, "bye," and turned and walked away. The bagman swung his arm around the old man's shoulders, and the two of them struggled to catch up with the preacher and the prostitute.

The four remaining seekers climbed a gentle slope up and out of the woods to a clearing littered with bottleglass and sun-faded cans that had once held soup and chili beans and beer and potted meat. The flames stretched to the horizon. Directly in front of the pilgrims lay a field of dry grass and dirt. Every-thing was coated with ash — each blade of grass and dandelion leaf, rocks already scorched by years of lonely cook fires — as if a decade of dust had been allowed to collect overnight in a doorless, breezeless room. Here and there flames danced in pockets where cinders had drifted on the wind and ignited the weeds. Across the field the avenues reached outward, endlessly straight, the buildings that lined them crackling, folding and falling to the flames. In the distance, the flames jumped high into the sky, leaping from rooftop to rooftop, expanding their dominion with every breath of wind. The ground shook with a thud as somewhere out of sight a gas truck exploded.

The pilgrims stopped. The bagman unburdened himself and dropped his bags on the ground. The old man began to cough again. He had to sit. "Oh shit," he said, shaking his head at the burning earth spread out before them, chortling between wheezes, "I take back everything I ever said."

The prostitute, who had been trailing her usual safe dis-tance behind, stood suddenly in front of the three men. She did not stop there and did not hesitate, but straightened her skirt and her halter top and with great dignity walked straight off across the field toward the flames. A spasm of coughing bent the old man in two. The preacher nodded to the bagman. His eye twitched, and his nose, and his cheekbones one by one, but he did not stutter when he spoke. "Come on then," the preacher said.

The bagman did not respond, so the preacher turned and followed the prostitute towards the fire. He lifted the bullhorn to his mouth and began to preach into the smoke in a smooth and even voice. "The steadfast love of the lord never ceases," the bagman heard him expound. "His mercies never come to an end." He watched the two of them recede into the distance, skirting the flames that blossomed in the reeds. He stared at the words written on the back of the preacher's sandwich board until they grew too small for him to read them. Beside him, the old man clutched his chest and retched.

The bagman could not take his eyes from the flames. From how they skipped and flared and faded. They had no fixed substance. They rose and fell according to the logic of their own hunger for air and for fuel. They would eat until there was nothing left to eat, and then they would be gone. There was nothing to them — nothing save heat, compulsion and a certain deathly beauty — yet at the moment they were everything. Fire — he realized, like the stranger he'd been seeking and like the paper-wrapped parcel the stranger had clutched to his bony chest, and perhaps like nothing else — was exactly what it was. But it could give him nothing, and he wanted nothing from it. This epiphany did not feel like a victory, and the bagman felt no freer for it.

The old man wheezed and collapsed against his shins. The bagman heaved him up into his arms. The old man's head lolled. He was lighter than a single bag. Without looking back, the bagman walked off with this new burden, back toward the city, away from the smoke and away from the fire. He left his bags in the clearing for the fire to claim.

I still can't sleep.

Flowers, it has been mentioned once or twice, are beautiful. So are stars and storm clouds, mountains and meadows, the flight of birds, the saddest songs, spiderwebs pulsing with struggling prey. Perhaps there is no need for reconciliation. Why should a foul breeze contradict a sweet one? Couldn't there be room for both? For everything? Creation is not a syllogism and cannot be divided. Or subdivided. It is, as any acid-tripping teen will tell you, all one. But one what?

I wait for the stranger. He doesn't come. He's not there in the mirror when I shave in the morning. He's not there at night when I brush my teeth. I don't find him on the couch in my office or the couch in my living room. He doesn't stop me in the street. I don't see him on my porch. He doesn't track mud through the hall. I look, but I don't find him. I look for him among the faces on the street, in cars stuck in traffic, in line at the market, on park benches and stoops. I see him nowhere.

I lie in bed. She sleeps beside me. The sheets feel heavy. Her breaths are even, long and slow. She hasn't had a nightmare in days. Her eyelids are fluttering, so I suppose she's dreaming, but I still can't see her dreams, if they're scary or sweet or something else. If I'm in them as well as in this darkened room.

I listen to the wind. It has been blowing all day. It whistles and shouts, makes the leaves rustle as if the sea's outside my door, waves lapping at the windows, begging to come in. I still can't sleep. Sometimes an empty can bounces along the asphalt, sometimes a big, hard plastic trash bin, protesting dumbly as it rolls.

He ignores the dragonflies.

She woke with his hands on her throat. The stranger kneeled on top of her. His thumbs were pressed against her larynx, but he did not squeeze. His eyes were red, and focused on some spot midway between her face and his. She lifted herself up on her elbows. His hands fell away. She took one of them in one of hers, smiled up at him with wide green eyes and kissed his palm. The stranger yanked his hand away as if she'd burned him. He struggled to his feet, turned, and almost fell through the door.

He sat in her small yard for hours, his eyes pressed shut, squatting among the dusty-shouldered dolls, wrapped in a blanket like a crone. The dolls, unimpressed, stood motionless. From all sides, sirens sang. Ash still fell from the sky. Even at noon, the sunlight filtered through the smoke a strange, dark violet. She squatted at his side and tried to draw his attention to two dragonflies, joined one to the other and flying together as one doubly thoraxed beast from bush to bush, carving wide, clumsy circles and wavering lines between the heavy flakes of ash. She laid her palm on his shoulder and pointed to the insects as they settled on a branch, then swam in lazy arcs across the sky, then stilled their wings and plunged towards the earth, pulling up and out of their freefall only millimeters above the ground. A low giggle rose from deep in her lungs, but the stranger did not look up.

She left him to go off foraging for food, and then returned, her pockets stuffed with chicken wings, an avocado, three bananas on their way from bruised to mush, an English muffin and more pears. Her face and hands and ankles were dark with smoke and ash. Her eyes, though, held no trace of shock or even unease at the recent transformations of the landscape, only joy at being by the stranger's side again. She found him no longer perched among the dolls, but crouching beside the warped particleboard wall of her shack, the blanket still pulled around his narrow back. Between his legs he held a battered and handleless saucepan, filled with water from the pipe. The stranger stared down at his reflection, his eyes red-rimmed and lost in their own wavering image.

Later that night, long after she had blown out the kerosene lamp and stretched out to sleep, the stranger's fingers trembled still. Again he wrapped them around her sleeping throat and placed one thumb over the other atop the small hillock of her larynx. This time he did squeeze. She couldn't scream of course, but neither did she struggle. Her arms remained at her sides. Her legs tensed, but did not rise to kick him. A gagging sound burbled up from somewhere near the center of her throat, not so different from her laughter. He tightened his grip, and stared down at her. But what did the stranger see?

Perhaps he saw that weightless spark of life that illuminated the woman's eyes even in the darkness. Maybe he saw her trust. Or perhaps he saw in her eyes the same puzzlement he had earlier that day seen floating in his own reflected gaze. Maybe it was love he saw, or something like it — something so contrary to all rational appetite, to all informed experience, to any reasoned calculus of what the world was owed, that it tripped him, and he fell. He let her go.

The woman coughed. A strand of drool leaked from her mouth, and tears leaked from her eyes. She did not wipe them away, did not even lift her hands to rub her throat. She lay still, and stared at him, her gaze expressing something more like pity than reproach. He stared back until tears rolled down his cheeks also, and he hid his face in his hands. His lips quivered. He sputtered out the words *I can't*. He choked and coughed and mouthed the word *forgive*, the words *forgive me*. He did not speak those words aloud, but that did not matter, as the woman could not hear. And though the room was too dark for her to see his mouth, she felt a tear fall warm from the tip of his nose onto her bare throat, and she lifted her palm to his face, to wipe his tears away and comfort him. The stranger took it like a slap. He leapt from the bed and ran naked into the night.

The sky had cleared of smoke. The stars stared down, hard and blue and far away. The stranger ran, and kept on running.

* * *

Unclothed, the stranger ran off into the burning world. I don't believe we'll hear from him again. There are those who cannot offer forgiveness, those who can't accept it. And those, like our brokedown hero, whose pride is so great and so fragile, that to even once lower themselves to beg forgiveness can be sufficient to destroy them. I pray that I am not so proud.

I sit at my desk, feet crossed beneath my chair, my papers again neatly stacked around me. The couch is empty. The dictionary closed, returned to its place on the shelf between the thesaurus and a field guide to common birds. Speaking of which, this morning a pigeon landed on my windowsill. Purple-headed, it turned two times with tiny, almost dainty steps incommensurate to its rounded bulk, and began preening its fat and feathered self. Then it noticed me less than a yard away on the other side of the glass, and flew off in panicked flurry. But the pigeons have long since gone to sleep wherever pigeons sleep. Perhaps on someone else's windowsill. It's a Tuesday and it's night already, so no one is preaching in the park. I hear only the usual sirens, the usual calamities. The ordinary apocalypses that join to make a day. Fires and floods, the tragedies of field mice and birds with broken wings. A fright suffered by a pigeon. A fruit fly's lonely death. The giantness of love. The smallness of our bodies. We eat and hope to mate. Hunger flows through everything. Call it whatever you like. Call it love if you prefer. The earth keeps spinning, a world among worlds among worlds, and all of them expanding, all of them reaching out for something else. Nothing begins and nothing ends. There are no boundaries to anything. To any things.

But I have to end this story somewhere. Soon I'll print this page and stack it with the others. I'll listen to my computer cease to hum. I'll watch the monitor blink dim. I'll get up, switch off the light, turn my key in the lock, wait for the elevator, lose patience, take the stairs. I'll go home, walk the cracked concrete path from the sidewalk to the porch, unlatch the gate, turn my key in yet another lock, pull the door closed behind me. I'll pull it closed on all of this and, forgive me, on you as well. Maybe she'll be awake.

Here the story ends. Somewhere else, others carry on. I told the stranger once that this wasn't about him anymore. That may have seemed cruel, but I was being kind. The truth is, it never was. There's always somewhere else. Look there instead. Somewhere else, not far, the bagman struggles to breathe life into the old man's age-worn lungs. Somewhere he fails. Somewhere the old man lets out a final cough that just may have been a laugh. Somewhere the bagman tries to walk unburdened. Somewhere a little fat boy washes the soot from his hands and face and constructs a sandwich for his grandmother: ham, tomato, mustard, no grubs. Somewhere a girl with long hair finds her father's car again, wipes the ash from its windshield and wonders what she's wished for. Somewhere three bald men wrestle in the embers. Somewhere Pigeon can't stop weeping. Somewhere the fires burn. They won't burn long. Somewhere else it rains. This is nothing new, no end and no beginning. These things happen all the time. Somewhere the deaf-mute sits among her troop of dolls, her hands crossed in her lap, and wonders what, if anything, she's lost. She tries to think of water and the surface of the sea. Somewhere already the wind blows hard and clears the ash and smoke from the sky. The stars shine bright above her. Some are blue, some are yellow and some are almost red. Some are hard and some are blurred. Some are not stars at all, but other planets and the moons of other planets, satellites, reflective trash that spins and spins. The moon winks. An owl hoots. A hummingbird sleeps hidden on a branch. A bullfrog belches love into the breeze. The stars shiver around her shoulders. Some are far and some are close. Some are very close. She reaches out and grabs one. It's too hot to hold. She tosses it from palm to palm and lobs it back into the sky. She grabs another, and she tosses it to you. Don't just sit there. Catch.★

★

★

★

★

★

★

★

★

★

★

★

★

★

★

★

★

★

★

★

★

★ Too slow. You let it fall! The star crashes to the floor, explodes. Fire races everywhere. Again the whole world burns. The page burns, the paper, the ink. The story burns. My computer burns. Magnetic zeros and ones flashing, sparking, sputtering out. The acrid smell of plastic melting, of zeros burning, melting. Flames trot across the carpet. They climb the mini-blinds to the camera on the wall. The walls burn. My office burns. And the broken elevator and the stairs and the bathroom down the hall. Bricks and concrete blocks aflame. The park burns, and the lake in the park and the pitted asphalt of the street. Even the potholes are burning. So I stay on the sidewalk, safe. I'm no fool. Or at least not that kind of fool. The buses are burning, so I have to walk. Sometimes I run to avoid the racing flames, to avoid burning up like the streets and the buses and the birds blazing through the sky like comets. I climb the hill, which of course is burning, and pass the bakery, also burning, and the neighbors' houses, all aflame. Only my house is not burning. It's fine, undamaged, sitting squat and stucccoed on its hillside beside the burning streets and all the burning houses and even the sky on fire now, the space between the stars on fire so that the entire sky is just one star, one big sun, one great celestial flame from horizon to horizon, except that the earth is burning too—every square inch of it save my house and the sidewalk in front of it—so what does it mean to talk of horizons anymore? Of up or down, here and beyond? What does it mean to talk of anything but burning? They're all there, gathered on the sidewalk, all of them. The stranger, the bagman, the deaf-mute, the old man, Pigeon, the preacher, the long-haired girl, the four nasty little boys and the fat boy's grandma, the three bald-headed men, the twin cripples, Martha also known as Marty, Gabriel, Michael, the prostitute, the man with the eye patch, all of them, even the woman with whom I share a bed. She's awake, standing off to the side and smiling, her arms crossed and her head tilted back and to the side like she's waiting for me to kiss her, or ask her to dance. They all look better. The bagman's wearing khakis and a V-neck cashmere sweater and his hair is trim and shiny with pomade. He looks a little lost still, but he smells like soap now, like Dove and Prell, and he's not carrying any bags. The old man is young again. He's wearing a shortstop's uniform, spitting tobacco juice into the dirt, winking. Pigeon is laughing, clowning, jumping up and down. His mom is with him. She tells him to quit fooling, but there's a softness to her voice and you can tell she doesn't mean it. The three bald-headed men have let their hair grow out. They're wearing turtlenecks, and reading Rilke. The long-haired girl has a buzz cut now. She's smoking Marlboros and glowing with tough, solitary cool. The stranger's wounds have healed. His suit is white again, and flawless. His beard is white too and there's an odd sort of gleam to him. He's standing behind the deaf-mute woman. His arms are wrapped around her waist. He's kissing her neck and whispering in her ear. Shock 'n' awe, he's saying, Shock 'n' awe, and he's nibbling at her earlobe and she's giggling and squirming and struggling to turn and kiss him back — she's not deaf anymore, or mute — but he's faster than she is and that's the game he's playing, to kiss her and love her and pretend not to let her love him back. I'm on the porch. It's funny, because I'm out here on the sidewalk with the rest of them, but I can see myself there on the porch as well, struggling with the latch on the gate, trying to get out. I look smaller than I thought I did, and not just physically. I mean I'm every bit as tall as I always am, but from the outside, from here on the sidewalk looking at myself over there on the porch I'm somehow less imposing than I imagined. Maybe it's because I'm bent over, hunched fighting with the latch. What's wrong with it? The camera above the door blinks red, watching me watch myself. The flames crack and spit behind me and I can feel their heat on the backs of my legs and the stranger says, Come on, join us, and he sounds sincere, cheerful even, and all of them are smiling now, all of us are. We're waving our hands, encouraging him. Me. Encouraging me. Come on, they say. Lift the latch, we say. Come join us. Lift it. He's trying. I'm trying. I want to help him but I can't seem to move. I'm watching myself trying, watching myself look up at all of us encouraging me, encouraging him, and I know he wants to join us, I want to join them out there on the sidewalk beside the burning street, but the latch is stuck, the gate is stuck, and they're not helping me, they're just standing there and I can't tell if they're mocking me or not, if they really want me out there or if they're just enjoying my clumsiness, my helplessness, but I don't care, I want to join them, to get through this gate to where I am and where they are, over there, looking so joyful in each other's company, but I can't. He can't. The latch is stuck. I can't get through the gate.

Acknowledgments

Details on moray eels and sea snakes were cribbed gratefully from Captain Michael Cargal's *The Captain's Guide to Liferaft Survival*. Any misrepresentations of those species are my own, and should not be pinned on Captain Cargal. The cockatiel's cry has been borrowed from an oration delivered by the heroic Mush Tate in chapter three of Edward Dahlberg's *Because I Was Flesh*. I am grateful to Elaine Katzenberger, Stacey Lewis, and everyone at City Lights.